Family Business

Book 1

Family Business Series

CH

Family Business

Vanessa Miller

Book 1
Family Business Series

Vanessa Miller
www.vanessamiller.com

Printed in the United States of America
© 2016 by Vanessa Miller

Praise Unlimited Enterprises
Charlotte, NC

Other Books by Vanessa Miller

Family Business Book I
Rain in the Promised Land
After the Rain
How Sweet The Sound
Heirs of Rebellion
Feels Like Heaven
Heaven on Earth
The Best of All
Better for Us
Her Good Thing
Long Time Coming
A Promise of Forever Love
A Love for Tomorrow
Yesterday's Promise
Forgotten
Forgiven
Forsaken
Rain for Christmas (Novella)
Through the Storm
Rain Storm
Latter Rain
Abundant Rain
Former Rain

Anthologies (Editor)

Keeping the Faith

Have A Little Faith

This Far by Faith

EBOOKS

Love Isn't Enough

A Mighty Love

The Blessed One (Blessed and Highly Favored series)

The Wild One (Blessed and Highly Favored Series)

The Preacher's Choice (Blessed and Highly Favored Series)

The Politician's Wife (Blessed and Highly Favored Series)

The Playboy's Redemption (Blessed and Highly Favored Series)

Tears Fall at Night (Praise Him Anyhow Series)

Joy Comes in the Morning (Praise Him Anyhow Series)

A Forever Kind of Love (Praise Him Anyhow Series)

Ramsey's Praise (Praise Him Anyhow Series)

Escape to Love (Praise Him Anyhow Series)

Praise For Christmas (Praise Him Anyhow Series)

His Love Walk (Praise Him Anyhow Series)

Could This Be Love (Praise Him Anyhow Series)

Song of Praise (Praise Him Anyhow Series)

Prologue

1971

Sliding into home plate Demetrius Shepherd knew that something had just gone real wrong. Trying to stop the opposing team from tagging him out, Demetrius did a crossover step with the right leg, then the back spike of the left leg caught in the clay and turned his foot completely around. He bit his lip, trying desperately not to cry. But honestly, he didn't know which was worse, the pain in his ankle, or the reality of knowing he wouldn't be able to finish out this state championship game.

Sam Johnson ran onto the field, he was screaming at people to get out of the way as he got down on the ground next to Demetrius, "You alright, son?"

Even with all the pain he was in, Demetrius smiled. He liked when Coach Johnson called him 'son'. Demetrius played baseball for Coach Johnson five years straight and each year he found himself wishing that the man had truly been his father. "It hurts coach."

"We're going to get you fixed up, just lay back and relax. This is not the end for you, Demetrius," Coach Johnson told him.

The team trainer ran onto the field, Coach Johnson got out of his way and then the trainer snapped his foot back in place... no tears, but he passed out as if he'd just received a knockout punch from George Foreman.

When Demetrius woke up, he was in the hospital with a cast on his leg. His father was standing next to his bed looking like one of his clients had just hit the number and he now had to pay up big time. Don Shepherd was the street numbers man. The lottery wasn't legal in Ohio, so Don was making a killing with his street numbers business. When his customers lost, Don won and won big. But he never liked paying when the shoe was on the other foot.

"What's wrong with you?" Demetrius asked. "I'm the one with the broken ankle."

"From what I heard, some dude was running up on you and that's why you slid wrong and broke your ankle."

Demetrius didn't want nothing to get started so he quickly said, "That dude was on the opposing team, Dad. He was supposed to tag me out, if he could. I just landed wrong. Nothing else to it."

"Well somebody's got to pay for what's been done to you." Don hit the wall with his fist as he angrily shook his head. "I am bound and determined to keep at least one promise that I made to your mama."

"I didn't break my good arm, Dad. I'll get some rehab on my ankle and then I'll be back on the field playing just like Tommy Davis back in '65."

"Tommy Davis was good. But he was never as good as he could have been if he hadn't broken that ankle. And the Dodgers knew it too. That's why they traded him as soon as they could."

Demetrius didn't want to hear all the reasons why not. Right now, as he lay in this hospital bed, feeling so much pain that he wanted to pass out again, Demetrius heard his coach telling him, "This is not the end for you." His father didn't believe in him. But his coach did and his mother had always believed in him, right up until the day she died.

When Demetrius was much younger, his dad had been a pimp and when money got tight he pimp out his own wife. Emma Shepherd had been too terrified of the six foot four semi-pro boxer to say no.

So, there were many nights when Emma would kiss her son goodnight and then head out to make that money. But some nights, before she hit the streets, Emma would get this tortured expression on her face and then she'd make Demetrius promise to stay in school and keep swinging that bat like no bodies business.

"I will, Mama. I promise," he told her, expecting to see her in the stands when he played his first professional game. But his hopes had been dashed when his beautiful mother was murdered by some deranged john who beat and stabbed her to death.

Demetrius had only been eleven when she died. He'd kept swinging that bat and running the field in hopes of going to college and then getting drafted into the Majors. Even though his mother was gone, Demetrius still wanted to make her proud. But with a broken ankle and a father who no longer believed in the dream, things weren't looking too good.

Don Shepherd stood up, he positioned his hands as if he were gripping a bat. As he swung it, he told Demetrius, "The next time you swing a bat, it'll be to collect on a debt owed to the family."

~~~~~

"Come on y'all, gather around 'cause I got something to say." At eight, Angelica Barnes was just a kid, but she already considered herself a minister-in-training. Her daddy was the most anointed preacher she'd ever seen and she figured she would need a lot of practice if she was going to be as good as Pastor Marvin R. Barnes III.

She waited as her brother and three friends from down the street were seated on the patio furniture. She then stood behind her makeshift podium and opened her Bible. "Since y'all don't know nothing about how to pray, I'm going to tell you what you need to do."

Ronny, Angelica's baby brother raised his hand and said, "I know about prayer. Daddy taught on it at church last Sunday."

"Hush up, Ronny," Angelica flipped a few pages in her Bible, she then turned back to her congregation with a stern expression on her face. "Turn in your Bibles to Luke, chapter 11."

The kids pretended to turn the pages, but really, they didn't know where to find Luke, Mathew, John or any of the Gospels for that matter.

Angelica began reading, "One day Jesus was praying in a certain place. When he finished, one of his dis... ci...ples said to him, "Lord, teach us to pray just as John taught his disciples." Sounding the word out. She said 'disciples' as best she could.

"He said to them, 'When you pray, say: Father, hallowed be Your name, Your kingdom come. Give us each day our daily bread. Forgive us our sins, for we also forgive everyone who sins against us. And lead us not into temptation."

When she was done reading she closed her Bible and said, "Do y'all know how to pray now?"

A little girl, a few years younger than Angelica said, "What does hallowed mean?"

Angelica tapped her index finger to her chin. "I've often wondered that myself. I'll ask my daddy and then I'll let you know."

The little boy seated next to Ronny then asked, "How can we live just on one piece of bread each day?"

"You're allowed to have more than a piece of bread," Ronny told him while shaking his head at his friend's question.

Angelica scolded her brother, "I'm teaching this lesson, so kindly allow me to answer all questions."

"But you don't know nothing," Ronny shouted back.

Angelica had had enough. Brothers were so stupid. She yelled, "Daddy, Ronny keeps interrupting me."

Pastor Marvin R. Barnes and his wife Maxine had been standing by the door listening to the sermon the entire time. They had to hold their mouths to quiet the giggling a few times, but nothing would have pulled them away from this vision of Angelica following in her father's footsteps.

"She's something, isn't she," Maxine said to her husband.

Marvin agreed. "I think we've got a preacher on our hands. Now let me help her teach this lesson."

Light shone all over Angelica's face as she beamed at her father. As far as she was concerned, her daddy being a pastor was just as good as being the president of the United States. "Thank you for helping me teach the Word of God to these kids, Daddy," she said as her captive audience jumped up and ran into the house.

"I enjoyed it." He took the Bible in his hands and sat down with her. There were tears in Pastor Marvin Barnes' eyes as he turned the pages to Jeremiah chapter 1. "As I walked out here, the Lord put something in my spirt for you, honey-bun."

"He did?" Angelica's voice was awestruck. How could she be on the Lord's mind? "What did He say?"

"Let's read it together." He held the Bible open to her. "It begins at verse five..."

"Before I formed you in the womb I knew you; Before you were born I sanctified you; I ordained you a prophet to the nations. Then said, I: 'Ah, Lord God! Behold, I cannot speak, for I am a youth'. But the Lord said to me: 'Do not say, I am a youth, For you shall go to all to whom I send you, and whatever I command you, you shall speak'."

As they finished reading, Angel looked to her father and asked, "What does it mean, Daddy?"

He lowered his head and kissed his daughter on the cheek. "It means that God has something special in store for you. So, you just keep doing what you're doing and always listen for the Lord's leading."

One

Ten years later…

"Let me go, Frankie. I'm done with this job and I'm done with you," a woman was yelling as Demetrius and Mo made their way up the alley.

Demetrius was thankful for the noise because it was leading him straight to the man they came to see. As they rounded the corner and rolled up on Frankie Day, Demetrius firmly held the bat that he used to practice with.

Frankie gripped the woman's arm with one hand and smacked her across the face with the other.

"I don't care if you beat me," the woman yelled. "Do whatever you want, but you're not going to make a whore out of me."

Demetrius couldn't see the girl's face because as they rounded the corner, they were facing Frankie's back and she was directly in front of him. But there was no fear in her voice, even after being struck hard. And Demetrius knew what fear sounded like. He'd heard it often enough from men who were supposed to be tough guys. But the minute he unleashed his beat down, things changed.

"You a stripper, Angel. You act like I'm asking you to do something you ain't never heard of."

"I won't do it," she said.

Frankie shoved her and then lifted a fist, getting ready to strike her again, but that's when Demetrius grabbed Frankie's arm and swung him around. "Didn't your mama tell you that boys aren't supposed to hit girls?"

Frankie's fist balled so he could strike out at the intruder. But once he caught sight of Demetrius, he backed up. "Hey man, you coming out to see my girls tonight…drinks on me."

As Demetrius grabbed Frankie, Mo held onto the woman, making sure she didn't run off and warn any of Frankie's boys. But somehow, Demetrius doubted that she wanted to help Frankie. He glanced over at her, and for a minute he almost forgot why he was in the alley in the first place. It was her eyes… big, brown and sexy, Even sexier than that white teddy and that see-it-all robe she was wearing. That caramel coated skin and long flowing sandy colored hair went well with those eyes and that teddy.

Demetrius pulled his eyes away from her, trying hard to focus as he told Frankie, "Can't come in tonight. Daddy's got me here on business." He then lifted the bat and smacked it into his free hand.

"Don don't have nothing to worry about with me. Business is good. I'll have his money by the end of the night." Frankie then turned to the vision in white and said, "If I could stop chasing these runaway strippers."

From the conversation Demetrius overheard as they walked up, it sounded like Frankie wanted this girl to do more than just strip.

"I'm not running away, I quit," she said with fire in those brown eyes.

"You don't get to quit on me. I own you in more ways than one." He poked a finger at her chest. "Remember that."

She tried to spit on him, but Frankie moved out of the way and then leaped on her like he thought the boys were there to watch him deliver a beat down. But Demetrius wasn't having it. Frankie got off a right-handed blow to the woman's cheek, but then Demetrius swung that bat like he was going for a home run. Frankie yelled and then fell to the ground.

"Why'd you stop me? I'm trying to get her in line so I can earn the money I owe your daddy."

"We came here to beat you down, not watch you beat some defenseless woman." Demetrius was about to swing again.

Frankie lifted his hands while sitting up and scooting back against the brick wall of his strip club. "Don't do this Demetrius, I got the money."

Demetrius really wanted to keep pounding this fool. But if he beat Frankie rather than collect the money his father sent him after, then he'd have to deal with Don Shepherd and nobody in their organization wanted to deal with his daddy. "Where's the money?"

"That-that's what I been trying to tell you. I got ten thou." Frankie stood back up, but kept a distance between him and Demetrius. He pointed towards the vision in white. "And one of my VIPs is ready to give me the other five right now if Angel will spend the night with him. He's crazy about her, and is upstairs waiting while she's down here giving me attitude."

The girl's name was Angel. She looked like an angel, Demetrius thought to himself. Too sweet and pure to be getting beat down in an alley because she didn't want to be pimped out. Or maybe this was a regular fight Frankie and Angel had every week. Maybe she just didn't like the john who was so hot for her. "She can make five G's in one night?" Demetrius asked incredulously.

"I'm telling you, man, this dude has been begging to have Angel for months now. Angel don't go in for stuff like that so I've been saying no." He hunched his shoulders. "But I got this debt with your daddy. So, it's time for Angel to help me out for once in her life."

Demetrius glanced over at Angel, tears were streaming down her face. He turned back to Frankie and said, "You got the ten G's on you now?"

Frankie pointed behind him, indicating the strip club which was nothing more than an old house, turned into a speakeasy/strip club. "In my safe. I was going to bring it around later tonight once I collected the rest of the money."

Demetrius directed Mo to go into the club with Frankie and collect the money. He then told them, "I'll stay right here with the money maker."

As Frankie and Mo headed inside, Demetrius eyed Angel from head to toe and back again. She was a vision of loveliness. Easily one the most beautiful girls Demetrius had seen in a long while. Other women might have been more polished. But the girl standing before him had a few more years to go before anyone would ever consider her a full-grown woman. By then, Demetrius figured she'd outshine any woman. Even Diahann Carroll back in her day. "How old are you?"

"I'm almost nineteen?" she answered while wiping the tears from her face.

"So, you're eighteen." Demetrius shook his head. "Why aren't you at home, letting your mama teach you how to cook, so you can land a husband or something?"

Restoring her tough girl exterior, Angel told him, "I'm going to mind my own business, and let you do the same."

"Oh, Okay." Demetrius put his hands up, indicating he was backing off. "Alright Ms. Mind-my-own-business. You don't seem to be doing such a good job of that, seeing as how you were just being slapped around in this alley."

"What do you know about it?"

Demetrius sat down on the stoop. "I might not know much about your situation, but if it was me, I sure wouldn't be in this alley when Frankie returned."

"I can't just leave."

Demetrius' eye brow lifted. He didn't understand this woman. Maybe she was just pretending that turning tricks bothered her. After all, she was a stripper… already getting paid for showing it, why not sell it all. "Hey, I tried to offer you a way out of this mess, but if you don't want to take it and run… then I'm going to sit over here and mind my own business like you suggested."

Angel glanced around the alley as if trying to find a way out. Her feet shuffled, then she turned to Demetrius and said, "I do want to go, but his sister babysits my kid. If I don't do what Frankie wants, he'll never let my baby go."

The tears were back, and even though she wiped them away quickly, Demetrius' heart was melting for her. It was like he wasn't seeing Angel, but his own mother, desperate to get out of a life that would kill her and take her away from him. He wasn't going to let another child endure the same pain he endured because some low-life decided to treat his mother like she was nothing and could be handled any kind of way.

"Okay, here it is," Frankie said as he and Mo came back into the alley. He handed Demetrius a stack of cash. "Count it if you want, ut it's all there."

"Not all," Demetrius said as he pointed toward Angel. "We still need that five thou."

"Problem with that," Frankie kept his eyes on Demetrius' bat as he said, "Dude got tired of waiting and left. But if you give me another week, I'll make sure that Angel works overtime to get that money."

"I'm not working another second for you. I just want to get my son and I'll be on my way."

Frankie reared back, getting ready to hit Angel again, but Demetrius grabbed his arm. "I told you already that we didn't come here to watch you beat on some woman."

Frustrated Frankie said, "Don wants his money. I'm trying to get it for him."

"I think I can help you out with that," Demetrius said. "I'll take the money you just gave me to my dad and then we will clear the books."

"Just like that?" Frankie asked in a tone that indicated he didn't believe Demetrius. "You're just going to forget about that other five?"

"Yeah, it's forgotten, no problem." Demetrius then pointed at Angel and said, "but I want her." He kept his eye on her as if she were a prize that he was bound and determined to win.

"What do you mean... for the night?"

Demetrius shook his head, still staring at Angel. "For good. This is her last night working for you anyway. So, from now on, she's with me."

"Now hold on, Demetrius. Angel is worth a lot more to me than five thou. The most I could do is rent her out to you for about a week. That's it."

Demetrius shook his head. "Take it or leave it. But just know that once I leave, you will be dealing with Don from here on out." He signaled for Mo to follow him, and twirled his bat as he headed out of the alley.

Mo caught up with him and whispered, "Don is gon' be ticked about this. We can't leave here without breaking an arm or a leg at least."

"I got this," Demetrius silenced Mo.

They kept walking, while Demetrius silently counted down "… 5… 4… 3… 2…"

"Hold up," Frankie called out to him. "Go on and take her, she ain't been nothing but trouble to me lately."

Angel didn't move, she looked from Demetrius to Frankie, as if she was unsure which devil would do her the most harm.

Then Demetrius said. "Come on Angel, I'll take you to pick up your son."

Angel still didn't move, she turned to Frankie, her eyes seemed to plead with him, "Can I take DeMarcus?"

Frankie glared at her with hatred building in his eyes. He practically spat at her as he said, "I don't care what you do, just don't come crawling back here once Demetrius is through with you."

He didn't have to tell her twice. Angel rushed over to Demetrius and got in the passenger seat while Mo climbed in the back.

Driving down the street, Mo told Demetrius, "I don't like this, man. Heads are going to roll when we get back to Don. He is not going to like that you bought some chick rather than collecting the rest of his money."

"This ain't on you, Mo. I can handle Don… besides, he owes me one."

~~~~

Saul's hawking form glided over the alley. He had one assignment for the night and it had been completed. Now he turned his big flapping wings and went up, up, up until he reached his heavenly home. As his feet touched down, his wings closed and his bejeweled sword could be seen as it hung from the belt strapped to his waist all the way to the tip of his foot.

Heaven had three parts, the inner court, the outer court and the Holy of holies where the throne of God resides. Saul made his way to the outer court where Captain Aaron stood in the midst of legions of angels, sending some out and welcoming others back home. Saul saluted his captain and then announced, "It is done my Captain. The two have met."

"Now the hard work begins," Captain Aaron told him.

"And these two are meant to be together?" Saul questioned. from what he saw of them, it seemed like a train wreck. But he wasn't God Almighty, so he didn't have any answers for the fallen humans.

"You may not have the answers," Captain Aaron said, cutting into Saul's thoughts. "But the child that will know both the truth of God and the ways of the street. He shall not only bring his family to Christ, but he shall be the one to usher in the last day revival, that will rock a nation and bring more souls to Christ than any other revolution the world has ever known."

"I do not understand it, my Captain, but I am your willing servant. You tell me where to go and what to do and I will protect these two with everything I've got."

"You have fought and won many battles, Saul. But, even you will need help with this assignment. You see, the child's life will be in danger even before he is born. The battle will be great, but if you and the other angels are able to dispatch the enemy, then revival will come to a nation that greatly needs it."

"And if we don't… I can't imagine the world getting any worse than it is now."

Captain Aaron put a hand on Saul's shoulder. "It will get much worse, my friend. So, you must protect Angel and Demetrius. And when it is time, protect the child, Tolbert, until the very end; for he shall proclaim the truth of God."

Lifting his sword, Saul pledged, "I will fight, and we will win; you have my word, Captain."

Two

"You did what? Boy quit playing and rush me the rest of my money," Don Shepherd looked like a body builder on steroids as he towered over his son.

"You heard what I said. I paid for Angel's freedom and that's that." Demetrius had towed the line and did everything he'd been told to do for most of his life. His father told him to quit baseball, even though he knew how much Demetrius loved the game… and he did it. He was told to join the family business, and without question, Demetrius suited up. But he wasn't budging on this one.

"You spent my money on a hooker?" Don was close to exploding.

Demetrius didn't care that his father was angry. He shrugged as he said, "It needed to be done."

Mo stepped back, not wanting any part of this. He positioned himself close to the door.

Don turned away from his son as if he was walking away from the situation, but then he quickly pivoted and back handed Demetrius so hard that the boy almost broke his wrist trying to break his fall. Don stood over him, glaring down as he said, "When I send you to do something, you get it done."

Mo put his hand on the door knob, opened it and tried to scoot out of the room, but Don wasn't having it. Without even looking his way, Don said, "Close that door and sit yourself down."

Mo did as he was told, while Demetrius wiped the blood from his lip. He then tried to stand back up, but Don put a foot on his chest. "I'm not through with you."

"It's over dad. I'm not giving the girl back. You can take the money out of my pay if it matters so much, I don't care." Demetrius had never challenged his father before, so he had no idea what Don Shepherd would do when he didn't show up with all of his money. But the truth of the matter was, he really didn't care what happened to him, just as long as he could save Angel from Frankie.

Don eyed Mo. "Where's the girl?"

"Don't tell him," Demetrius screamed from his spot on the floor.

Mo screamed right back at him. "What else can I do, D, man? I told you this was a bad idea, but you wouldn't listen… talking about your daddy owes you one."

Don took his foot off of Demetrius' chest. He reached down, took a handful of Demetrius' shirt and pulled him to his feet. "I'm your daddy, boy. Without me you wouldn't even have life… so how do I owe you?"

Demetrius dusted himself off and squared his shoulders as he stood and faced off with his father. Which was a little hard to do since Don was two feet taller than Demetrius' 6'2 frame. "You weren't the only one who gave me life… I had a mother." Demetrius had the good sense to step back as he added, "and you took her away from me."

Don swung around, turning his back to his son. He shook his head and sucked in air. Don made his way to the bay window and stared off as if looking into a distant past that he hadn't allowed himself to think about for a very long time. He turned back to Demetrius as he said, "Your mama had been down for whatever I wanted or needed from the moment we hooked up. I loved her for that."

The room went silent. Demetrius and Mo glanced at each other, not knowing whether they should run or hide. But then Don got the coldest look in his eyes that Demetrius had ever seen. He said, "Okay, you got your little hooker, so consider my debt paid-in-full."

Demetrius and Mo headed for the door, but Don stopped them.

"Demetrius." He turned, looked at his father. "Don't you ever throw this in my face again. You got me?"

Demetrius nodded. "I got you."

~~~~~

Slamming his keys down on the counter as he entered his home, Demetrius punched the fridge, letting out his frustration. His dad had treated him like nothing more than hired help. He'd been loyal to Don Shepherd for ten years, doing his bidding. Whether it was number running or beating down the men who dared not pay back a loan, he'd been down with it. He'd never asked for special treatment simply because he was Don Shepherd's son. The one time he took a liberty, his father disrespected him and treated him like he was nobody.

Demetrius had half a mind to move and start up his own operation in another city. But as he stood there trying to decide which city to move his operation to, Demetrius slowly came to the realization that his father's arm was long and his connections were spread so wide that he'd never be able to set up shop without Don Shepherd getting wind of it. Slamming his fist on the counter, he practically growled throughout the house, "I hate him!"

Angel stepped into the kitchen with a worried look on her face. "Is everything alright?"

Demetrius glanced her way, he'd forgotten that he had brought her to his home.

Leaning against the fridge, Angel told him, "If you want me and DeMarcus to get our stuff and leave, it's cool. I appreciate what you did for us. But I don't want to be a burden to anybody."

"Did I say you was a burden?"

"No, but you don't look very happy." Then as she noticed something she rushed to Demetrius 'side and put her hand on his lip. "You've been bleeding. Let me get some ice."

"I don't need no ice."

Ignoring him, Angel took a few ice cubes out of the freezer and wrapped them in the kitchen towel. She placed it on Demetrius' lip, asking, "You got into another fight?"

"I wouldn't call it a fight."

"What would you call it then, because I can tell that you've been in a scuffle."

Demetrius shrugged. "Just my father's way of saying thanks for costing him five big ones."

Angel's hand flew to her mouth as she dropped the ice she was holding against Demetrius' lip. She bent down to pick up the ice. Dumping the ice in the sink. she said, "I'm so sorry for all the trouble I've caused. But I promise that I will find a way to pay you or your father ever cent that I owe."

Demetrius didn't know why he did it, but he put his arms around Angel's waist and pulled her close against his body. "You can start paying me back right now."

Shaking her head, Angel pushed away from him. "I'm not a whore, Demetrius. And I won't let Frankie, you or anyone else treat me like one." She turned away from him and went into the guest bedroom. She picked DeMarcus up off the bed and put his jacket on. The boy was still asleep so it took a little longer to get his things on. She then grabbed her purse and the two bags of clothes she'd brought to the house with her and started heading for the door.

"Hey, where are you going?" Demetrius caught her before she could get out of the door.

"We're leaving," Angel told him with fire in her eyes.

"How? Are you going to walk?"

"I'll catch the bus."

Demetrius didn't understand this at all. He thought Angel didn't have any place to stay, that's why he told her to come to his house. Now she was ready to leave, like she had a house on the hills or something. "I thought you didn't have a spot."

"I don't. Frankie's sister had been letting me crash on her couch so I could save up enough money to get a place."

"Well you can't go back over there. Frankie'll put you on the stroll for real this time."

She smirked as she looked up at him. "It sounds like you want me to be a working girl up in here, so what's the difference?"

Her words made him feel slimy. Like he was no better than Frankie or his father. He didn't like that feeling. He'd never forced himself on a woman in all of his twenty-seven years and he wasn't going to start now. "There isn't a shortage of women out there. You don't want to be with me, fine... I'm not sweatin' it. You can work off your debt to me by keeping the house clean and making sure I got dinner ready when I come home."

Looking around the room at all the fast food bags and soda bottles that had been left in the living room, Angel scrunched her nose and nodded. "This place could use a good cleaning."

25

"What can I say, my housekeeper quit." He grabbed her bags and headed back to the guest room with them as he slung them over his shoulder, "You can cook, can't you?"

Grinning from ear-to-ear, Angel told him, "I can make homemade biscuits and the best fried chicken and collard greens you ever tasted."

"Sounds good. Wish my mom had cooked like that... it was hamburger helper and stove top stuffing."

"My mom didn't work outside of the home, so she loved cooking from scratch and teaching me to do the same," Angel said as she followed Demetrius back to her bedroom.

He put her bags back down as he said, "Yeah, that was the problem. My mother was always working; my dad made sure of it."

Three

"Where to today," Mo asked as Demetrius took a seat on the passenger side of his Jeep.

"Number running duty today, my man. So, we gotta be real nice to the customers we have left. The government legalizing the lottery in Ohio and adding that pick 4 option has hurt business."

Mo glanced over at Demetrius. He had this whatever look on his face. "I'm nice to all my customers, no matter what. But I must admit, this lottery has trimmed our profits."

"Now if one of our customers hits, daddy be acting like they stealing from him."

"Remember when Mr. Homer won twenty thou, and Don started stuttering, and then slammed his fist in the wall before he finally coughed up the money."

"I remember," Demetrius laughed. "Don had to wrap his hand for a month like he was still boxing."

Demetrius was laughing on the outside, but this was something very real and personal to him. After his father had finished boxing with the wall, Demetrius had told him that paying the money was non-negotiable. He'd never questioned his father's integrity on these deals before. But it was getting harder to make ends meet and none of his clients had ever won that much money… and none of them were like Mr. Homer.

Demetrius was normally in and out of client's homes. Sometimes he just took the numbers on the porch, they handed him the money for their bet and then he was on his way. But Mr. Homer was different. He was a baseball fan and had seen Demetrius play when he was in high school. Mr. Homer had even given him a Willie Mays baseball card. And even though Jackie Robinson and Hank Aaron were his favorite all time baseball players, Demetrius treated that card like it was a piece of gold.

Mo pulled up in the parking lot of the Church's Chicken on Riverview and got out of the car. He told Demetrius, "We can eat here when we get done with our route."

Demetrius shook his head. "Not today. I've got a meal waiting on me when I get back home."

"You gon' keep her up in the house, huh?" Mo smirked. "Since you almost got the both of us killed over that girl, I sure hope you planning to share."

"She's not like that, man. Angel's in my guest room. She cooking and cleaning my house to pay me back the money I lost on her."

"You really think your daddy is going to hold your money?" Mo didn't look as if he believed that.

"Sure do. So, I might as well get something out of this deal… I haven't had a woman cooking and cleaning behind me since my mama died."

"That's because you never wanted anyone in your house. So, why you all of a sudden trust this girl?"

Demetrius didn't want to explain his reasoning, because in truth, helping Angel felt more to him like he was helping his own mama. He had finally put his foot down and not allowed some man to send a woman somewhere that might get her killed. Demetrius didn't want Angel's son to carry the pain of missing his mother, because he knew how that felt. "She's cool people. I can deal with her and her son for a little while."

They arrived at the first house. Demetrius knocked on the door as Mo said, "Be careful, that girl will have you over there playing daddy to her son in no time."

"Who?" Demetrius laughed at that. "I ain't got no kids and ain't trying to have any no time soon."

~~~~~

Angel had written out a grocery list the night before and handed it to Demetrius before she and DeMarcus went to bed for the night. The next morning the refrigerator and the cabinets were fully stocked. Angel got down to the business of cleaning, and from what she could see, Demetrius truly needed her services. Humming as she worked, Angel even smiled as she took out the trash. Housekeeping might not pay much, but it was an honest day's work and wasn't nobody asking her to 'take it all off, baby'.

Just as Angel thought of her short lived life as a stripper, DeMarcus started crying in his sleep. Angel put the broom down and picked her baby up. Rocking him as she kissed his forehead, Angel told him, "Don't you worry little fellow, I'm not going back to that place ever again. I promise you that."

Some days Angel wished she had never left home... never met Frankie and then stupidly fell for all his lies. And some days Angel held onto the anger she felt for her cousin who had worked at Frankie's club, and told Angel how wonderful the life of a stripper was... and how much money she was making. She hadn't bothered to mention how much shame she would feel each time she took her clothes off in front of strangers.

She had been stupid. Angel had no business being around street people, because she hadn't known anything about the lifestyle before she ran away from home. Frankie had been so smooth that she hadn't recognized him for the devil he was. Angel wished she could go home and see her mother and brother, she missed them so much. But how could she explain that she now had a son with no husband?

She put her son back down and then went into the kitchen to start dinner. She'd decided that meatloaf, mashed potatoes and green beans sounded good. Once she put her food on, Angel started on the bathrooms. Demetrius had two. One in the hallway and the other in his bedroom. Angel was a bit leery about going into his bedroom at first. But she didn't want Demetrius thinking that she was slacking on any part of her job. She stepped into his bedroom and was immediately surprised by what she saw. The bed was a mess of course, so she stripped it and put his sheets in the washing machine.

However, the thing that left her in awe was the huge black and white pictures that hung on his walls. She doubted these men were family members because they were all dressed in baseball gear. The pictures reminded her of Demetrius swinging that bat in the alley and then Frankie holding his arm as if it was broken. "The boy likes his baseball," she said to herself as she went into the bathroom and cleaned until it shined.

As she closed his bedroom door, Angel smiled at how nice the home was beginning to look. She doubted that cooking and cleaning would be enough to pay Demetrius everything that she owed. But, she was still going to do the best job possible. She also planned to look for another job, so she could earn money to pay this debt. But this time she wouldn't settle for a job that required her to take her clothes off.

The thing Angel didn't understand was how she had fallen so hard, so fast. One day she was a little girl dreaming about following in her father's footsteps and the next thing she knew, she was running away from home, having a baby, and then becoming a stripper. How she wished things had turned out differently, but they hadn't and Angel blamed her parents for that.

They were the ones who'd given up and caused her to lose her faith and the feeling that all was right with the world. Now, Angel not only knew that there was evil in this world... she had slept with the devil.

Trying to get her mind off of her baby's daddy, Angel went back to the kitchen. She turned off the mashed potatoes and opened a box of Jiffy corn muffins. It was smelling good in the kitchen and Angel smiled as she tasted her meatloaf... delicious as usual. The secret, her mother taught her, was in the parmesan cheese and Italian sausage added to the meat mixture.Not to mention, the barbecue sauce rather than tomato sauce as the outer glaze.

The front door opened just as Angel was turning off the oven. She hollered to him, "Dinner's ready."

~~~~

"Mmmm, it smells good in here." Demetrius closed the door and made his way to the kitchen. Taking his jacket off, he slung it across the back of the chair. But Angel quickly snatched it off of the chair.

"You do have a hall closet, you know." She put his jacket on a hanger and hung it in his closet. "Wash your hands," she hollered at him as she walked back into the kitchen to fix his plate.

"Girl, you acting like my mama, rather than a housekeeper."

As Angel put the food on his plate she retorted, "I might not be your mama, but I still want you to wash your hands."

Rolling up his sleeves, Demetrius went to the sink and washed his hands. Angel put the plate in front of him as he sat back down.

She stood watching as Demetrius put his fork in the meatloaf, and then brought the fork to his mouth. She held her breath as he bit into it, and didn't release it until she heard him sigh.

"This is some good eats." Demetrius' cheeks puffed out as he stuffed his mouth with food. He swallowed the food on his plate and then asked for a second helping. As she was getting his plate, he asked, "Aren't you going to eat?"

"Not right now. I'm going to check on DeMarcus and then we'll eat something later."

She put the plate in front of him and then Demetrius said, "I can't eat all this good food alone. Why don't you get DeMarcus and the two of you can eat with me."

But Angel backed away from the table. "I didn't know that being your dinner companion was going to be a part of my job duties."

Putting his fork down, Demetrius glared at her. "There you go with that mess. I got plenty of people I can eat with, so don't worry about me." His beeper went off, Demetrius glanced at the number, then went to the wall phone in the kitchen and dialed the number.

"Hey man, what's up… Nothing, just eating."

Demetrius switched the phone from one ear to the next. He answered the caller's question by saying, "Sounds good. I don't have anything else to do tonight. Might as well go clubbing."

Demetrius listened a few moments, then he cut his eyes in Angel's direction as he said, "Instead of meeting me at the club, won't you come through. My housekeeper made dinner, and it is good."

Her back was to him when he called her a housekeeper, so he couldn't see her face, but he saw those shoulders tighten. Serves her right, Demetrius thought. If she wanted to be treated like an employee, he would do just that.

Four

From that night on, Demetrius brought one or two of his friends home with him for dinner. Angel didn't mind though. While Demetrius and his friends ate dinner, she would play with DeMarcus or wash clothes. She kept the house together and they stayed out of each other's way. But one night, after a long day of cleaning, washing and folding clothes, Angel fell asleep on the sofa.

She didn't know how long she had been out, but when she woke up, a pillow was under her head and a blanket was thrown across her body. She was rubbing her eyes, trying to get her bearings, when she heard DeMarcus say, "Dadda, Dadda."

DeMarcus had been sound asleep in their bedroom when she sat down to fold a load of clothes, but now it sounded as if he was in this very room with her. He was sixteen months, so he was in that scrawl-walk phase. Angel tried her best to keep an eye on him, because it only took one wrong move for a baby to get hurt. Her mother had experienced that with Ronny. The boy had always been curious, always getting into things. One day he decided to climb the wooden fence in the back yard. If she hadn't found him when she did, Ronny would have discovered that the fence had been erected to keep children from falling into the steep, rocky creek below.

As if coming out of a nightmare, Angel's eyes darted around the room. That's when she saw DeMarcus climbing all over Demetrius as he sat on the love seat. "I must have fallen asleep," she said as she leaned over and grabbed DeMarcus.

"Daddy," DeMarcus said again as he reached for Demetrius.

"Sorry about that, he's just confused," she said of DeMarcus calling him daddy.

"No worries," Demetrius told her. "Oh, and I gave him a bottle when he woke up."

She looked around the room. "What happened to the clothes I folded?"

"I figured you needed a rest, so I put them in my dresser. Then DeMarcus and I sat down and started watching the game."

She thought it was odd that Demetrius would be doing her job when that was supposed to be her way of paying back the money she owed him. She was just about to tell him that, when a baseball player slid into home base. Demetrius jumped out of his seat and started whooping and hollering, as if he was seated in the stands rather than watching the game on the television in his living room. "What's the deal with you and baseball anyway?"

"I love the sport," he answered as he sat back down.

"Plenty of folks love the sport, but that don't mean they gon' put life size pictures of people playing baseball in their bedroom." Angel didn't get it. Could a person really be that much of a fan?

"Those people you're referring to are Jackie Robinson, Hank Aaron and Willie Mays; only the best ever players to come out of the Negro leagues." When she gave him a look that showed she still didn't get it, he said, "These Cats were fearless. Jackie Robinson broke the color barrier when he became the first black man to sign with a national baseball team.

35

"He practically led the way for Hank Aaron to break Babe Ruth's home run record. And Willie Mays is just Mr. MVP as far as I'm concerned."

Angel shook her head as she laughed at him. "Look how excited you get talking about baseball. It's a wonder you didn't play yourself."

That's when the laughter stopped, because as soon as the words were out of her mouth, Angel saw the look of sadness creep up his face. He looked so wounded that she wanted to put DeMarcus down and go to him. But she didn't want things to get weird or to have Demetrius thinking that she was offering anything more than her sympathy. So, she remained seated as she asked, "What's wrong? What did I say?"

He got up and turned off the television. "I'm going back out for a while. I'll see you and DeMarcus tomorrow."

"You're going to be gone all night?" Angel sounded outraged, as if she had a right to question Demetrius concerning his comings and goings.

"What's it to you? You've made it clear that I need to keep my distance. You don't even want me to touch your son."

"I never said I had a problem with you holding DeMarcus."

"Then why did you snatch him away from me the moment you woke up? Acting like I'm going to harm him or something, when I'm the one who gave y'all a place to stay. Where's his daddy anyway? Why didn't he come to your rescue?"

"You already know DeMarcus's daddy." She was embarrassed to have to admit that she had been with a man who didn't care about her, so she lowered her head as she added, "And that low-life wanted me to come to his rescue. He never once thought about doing anything to help me or his son, that didn't first help him."

Demetrius' eyebrows furrowed. "What do you mean, I already know him? Who is this guy? Does he know that you were stripping in order to make ends meet?"

"I can't believe you haven't figured this out already." She stood up, with DeMarcus on her hip and walked over to him. "Why do you think Frankie's sister was babysitting DeMarcus for me? Do you really think Frankie is providing babysitting services for all of his strippers?"

He looked puzzled for another moment, then blurted out. "You mean to tell me that this is Frankie's kid?"

"I wish I didn't have to admit to that. But it's true. The love of my life was trying to prostitute me, even though he knew that our son was at his sister's waiting on me."

Demetrius shook his head. "I knew Frankie Day was a piece of garbage, but I never would have pegged him like that." He grabbed Angel's free hand, walked her back towards the sofa and then sat down with her.

After a long moment of staring into her eyes, as if he was trying to read all of her secrets, he finally said, "I just don't get it."

Angel was confused. She had no clue where this was going. "Get what?"

"You seem like a smart girl, you sure don't have a problem letting a brother know what's on your mind... and you are really beautiful. I just don't understand how you could get hooked up with Frankie... were you already stripping when you met him, or what?"

She was slightly insulted by the question. But since Demetrius was responsible for the roof that was currently over her son's head, she felt that she owed him the truth, as painful as it was. "No, I didn't know anything about this sort of life when I met Frankie. I was as green as green could be."

"I left home at sixteen because I couldn't deal with all the drama my parents were going through. My cousin, Ramona, convinced me that she was living the high life out here, so I hopped on a Greyhound and met up with her. But I was only here a little over a month when Ramona got herself arrested for holding drugs for her low-life boyfriend."

DeMarcus climbed off the sofa and used a jar of lotion as a ball as he rolled it around on the floor.

Angel continued. "Before Ramona got arrested, she'd introduced me to Frankie… told me he was a nice guy who owned a gentlemen's club downtown." Angel laughed at the memory. "I had pictured well-dressed men going to a private club to smoke cigars and drink brandy. I honestly had no clue what she was talking about."

"And of course Frankie didn't explain it to you," Demetrius said, knowing full well how the game was played.

"When I first met Frankie, he kept promising to take care of me and to give me some so-called good life. I fell for his whole line, because I really had no choice once Ramona left. But after a while, I started catching on. I caught him cheating on me, and demanded that he stop. But that's when he had a surprise for me. He said that since I wasn't happy being his number one woman, that I would have to earn my keep like all the rest of 'em.."

"Why didn't you just go back home? I'm sure your parents would have let you come back. Wouldn't they?"

"My parents are divorced. They were too busy fighting and blaming each other to care about what happened to me and my brother." She shook her head as she added, "And they messed me up more than Frankie ever could. Because when I was young, my parents had me believing that life was this wonderful thing, and God was good all the time, and then they just snatched all of that away from me. I couldn't see any more goodness in our lives after they divorced." And even after being away from home for three years now, tears still floated around her eyes as she thought about what used to be.

"Sounds like things are bad for you no matter which way you turn."

Angel agreed.

"Well, I can promise you this, Angel," Demetrius stood up. "I ain't no wolf in sheep's clothing. I'm not going to make you do nothing around here but what we've already agreed on. And you and DeMarcus can stay as long as you need to." After those words he grabbed his keys and left.

~~~~

Don Shepherd called a meeting that night. Demetrius was still smarting over the way he had been treated, so he originally planned to skip it. But after sitting there staring into Angel's eyes, Demetrius knew he had to get out of the house. He wanted to kiss that girl so bad that he ached. But he would never let Angel know how he was feeling. He didn't want to scare her off. It was obvious that she needed someone in her corner who wasn't out to take something from her.

"Demetrius, do you want to join us over here?" Don asked his son.

No, he didn't want to join them anywhere, he wanted to be out on a baseball field hitting homers and hearing the crowd go wild as he made his way to home base. But even after all these years, his ankle still wasn't flexible enough for him to run on the baseball field without it kinking up on him. So, here he was at another one of his father's meetings and still doing nothing about the promise he made to his mother.

"It's some real serious stuff going down," Don told the group of five, who were all considered his lieutenants. "Leo Wilson and his boys have just been indicted. They wouldn't even set a bail for Leo. So he won't be running numbers or taking bets on the fights. Business has to keep rolling though, so Leo has asked for our help."

Don Shepherd was notorious in these parts and didn't nobody even think about messing with him. Because everybody on these streets knew that Don wasn't just the meanest hustler out there, he also had a little bit of crazy in him.

Even with all Don's crazy, Leo Wilson had remained the Head Negro in Charge. Don hadn't contested that fact, because Leo had been running the streets of Dayton, ten years before Don Shepherd came on the scene. Don respected the man; but that didn't mean that Don wasn't biding his time until he could take over, and once and for all, take his rightful place. So, it surprised Demetrius that Leo had turned to his father for help in his time of need.

"Joe Frazier's and Ali's fights both take place in December. With Leo gone, we have no competition and if we play are cards right, we can make a killing." Don clasped his hands together as if feeling the money as he continued, "Leo is handing over his contacts, so we need to get busy. As we all know, the government is running us out of the number running business. They're even proposing that the lottery proceeds help fund education. Now how can we compete with that?"

"I seriously doubt that any of them educational funds will make their way to our community. But this meeting isn't about them lottery jokers, so I'll just say this… if we make the right moves and don't make no mistakes, we just might be able to retire when it's all said and done."

"Why's Leo being so generous?" Stan Michael, Don's second in command asked.

"He wants us to break him off half of the proceeds," Don answered.

"Even though we getting ready to do all the leg work, and risk our necks on a hot contact list that the Feds are probably watching to see who bites first?" said Al Gamer, the lieutenant who all other lieutenants feared because he could smile at you, say good morning, put a bullet in your skull and then sit down and eat your breakfast.

Don loved Al's ruthlessness, and often put him to work against his enemies. Smiling as he answered his enforcer, Don said, "Oh my friend, you know me so well. I already told Leo that we were assuming too much risk for a fifty-fifty cut. So, he has agreed to take forty percent. At this point, Leo just wants to make sure that his family will be well provided for while he does his time."

His father sounded so benevolent with his talk about providing for another man's family and giving another hustler his cut. Demetrius just couldn't believe it. "So, you're going to help Leo out?"

Don glanced over at his son. The smile he had for Al was gone. "Why wouldn't I? Leo would do the same for me if I got jammed up like that."

"That's all good and everything," Stan said, "but when are we going to put aside this penny ante money we raking in and get in the dope game? You already said that the government has taken over the numbers business. So, let's just give it to them, and start raking in the real bread."

41

"Stan has a point," Al agreed, "Crack is blowing folks mind. I never seen people get strung out on something so fast."

Don looked at his son. "What do you think?"

"It's risky," Demetrius answered. His father had always told him that dealing heroin was out of the question because he feared becoming an addict himself. Crack was different because they weren't using a needle and putting that stuff in their veins. But it was just as lethal.

"No risk, no reward," Stan said.

Don thought about that a moment. He nodded. "We need to become distributors to these little corner dope men out on these streets. If we sit at the top, we get most of the reward and fewer risks."

Demetrius liked the sound of that. If he was making more money, then he would be able to stock pile enough loot to get out of this town. "I'm in."

"Without a doubt," Don said as he looked at his son as if Demetrius had no choice in the matter. "We are going to own this city. But we've got to earn enough money on these two fights before we can even think about elevating our business."

"If we get too many winners there's no way that we'll have enough money to pay them all and still be able to come up the way you talking about coming up," Joe-Joe said.

"Let's cross that bridge when we get there. For right now all we need to do is collect the bets. Make sure to talk up Frazier and Ali," Don told them.

Al laughed. "You gone crazy or something, Don? Everybody knows those two are way past their prime. They must be punch drunk to even think about getting back in the ring."

"They know what we tell them. And if you say you're putting your money on Ali or Frazier, most of them will too." Don rubbed his hands together while licking his lips in anticipation. "I'm telling you, we're gon' make a killing."

"Ali used to be like a super hero to me. But after that beating he took from Larry Holmes last year, I never thought he would get back in the ring." Al shrugged as if it was no water off his back. "If he's going to be stupid like that, I can't think of any other group of people I'd like to see get rich from it."

Five

"You leaving early again this morning?" Angel said as she threw on her housecoat while following Demetrius down the hall.

"Early bird catches the worm. Got to get out there and make my paper before somebody takes it from me."

"Ain't nobody taking nothing from you. Not as long as you Don Shepherd's boy." She grabbed hold of his arm and tried to pull him towards the kitchen. "Sit down and let me scramble some eggs."

But Demetrius snatched away. "I got a long day ahead of me."

"Want you just tell your daddy that you need some time off?"

Demetrius put a hand on the doorknob, but before he opened it, he turned back to her and said, "I'm nobody's boy, Angel. Everything I've gotten, I've scuffled and scrapped for."

"Scratch the attitude so early in the morning." Angel scowled at him. "It's not like I said you were Mo's boy. Don Shepherd is your father, remember?"

"Whatever." Demetrius snatched open the door. As he walked to his car he loudly mumbled. "I'm my own man. I ain't never been nobody's boy."

"Okay, Grumpy," Angel shouted at him as she closed the door.

Demetrius wanted to go back in the house and have it out with Angel. She got under his skin and he was tired of it. But he decided to get in his car and put distance between them. He needed distance from DeMarcus too. Because as much as he hated to admit it, he liked it when DeMarcus called him daddy. Liked it that the boy's name began with a 'D'. Because he wanted all of his sons' names to start with a D. "I am losing it," he told himself as he sped off.

Mo met up with him at the International House of Pancakes. Angel had been right about Demetrius needing to eat, because he was starving. But he wasn't about to sit in that kitchen while Angel pranced around in her robe acting like the little woman of the house. "You want to start on Williams street today?" Demetrius asked while stuffing a fork full of hot and syrupy pancakes into his mouth.

"Sounds good," Mo said. "Mr. Johnson told me to come by and pick up his money, so I can do that while we're over there."

Sam Johnson was a sixty-seven year old retired teacher. He had been Demetrius' Little League coach back when he was in school. "Why you collecting on Coach Johnson's numbers? He normally works with me."

Mo took a piece of Demetrius' toast, slathered butter on it and then took a bite. "Not getting money for numbers. Coach Johnson wants to bet on the fight... said he was going to take a bundle out of the bank so he could cash in."

Pushing the plate away, Demetrius wiped his mouth and then threw the napkin on it. "Don't matter whether its numbers or the fight, don't nobody deal with Coach Johnson but me."

Mo just shrugged. "Cool man; make sure you get over there. Don't want to miss out on that money because of slacking."

"I'll get to him." Standing up, he put some money on the table and said, "Let's get at it."

45

"Dinner at your place tonight?" Mo asked as they stepped out of the restaurant.

"Angel made some lasagna last night. We still have a big pan of it left, so come on through. I should be home at about seven." They fist bumped and then parted ways.

Most of Demetrius day was filled with numbers. One customer after the next had dreamed of these three numbers, or those three numbers, and just knew that they were getting ready to get paid. He had coffee with Thelma Green as he collected her numbers. "I got a good feeling about those numbers I picked today," Thelma told him as he stood to leave.

"What's so special about these numbers?" Demetrius played along.

"My dead grandmother came to me last night and whispered those numbers in my ear. She used to win big money playing the numbers, so I know she wouldn't have given them to me if those numbers weren't right. My hand was even itching this morning."

"I hope you win big, Thelma," Demetrius told her.

"Me too. That's why I cast my bets with you instead of with them white folks. Ain't no reason to give them one red cent."

Demetrius was thankful that Thelma was loyal like that. But in truth, times were changing. The lottery was taking over. Half of their customers had already stopped doing business with them. Maybe his father was right about it being time for them to get out of the business.

Just as Demetrius was thinking about their way out of the numbers business, Thelma called out to him. "Hey Demetrius, I almost forgot something." She ran over to his car and handed him twenty dollars. "Put that on Frazier. I've been hearing that he's got some come back in him."

"Will do, Thelma. Will do."

And on and on it went. Demetrius didn't even feel guilty about taking ten, twenty and hundred dollar bets on Frazier or Ali, even though he doubted that either of them could win against a good fighter at this point.

But when he got to Coach Johnson's home, things got real for him. Mr. Johnson had gone to the bank and pulled out ten thousand dollars. "I managed to save twenty thousand dollars before me and the misses retired. But that money don't mean nothing now that her arthritis done kicked in."

Demetrius shook his head. "I still don't think you should spend half your retirement money on a gamble that might not pan out. Remember what you used to tell us before each game?"

"Don't count your chickens before they hatch," Sam answered him. "But that was different. I didn't want you kids getting the big head and then going on that field and losing like suckas... My wife can't deal with this cold weather anymore. It makes her bones ache something terrible. So, we've been planning to move down South. And I need more than twenty thousand to do that."

"But don't you have family that you could rent a room from down South or something?"

Grinning from ear to ear, Coach Johnson said, "You remember Calvin, don't you?"

"Your son." Demetrius nodded. "He graduated high school my freshman year, but I remember him."

"He lives in South Carolina now. Got himself a wife and a good job down there. And they just made us grandparents. We want to buy a small house somewhere close to them. Katherine's been dreaming about babysitting and going on outings with our grand-daughter."

"Why don't you just stay with them?"

47

Coach shook his head. "We don't want to intrude on their lives. Anyway, you know how it goes. If you stay too long, you make the people glad twice... glad to see you come and glad to see you go."

Demetrius hated that Coach Johnson could possibly throw away half of his savings on a gamble that might back fire on him, but he wasn't the conscience police. It was his job to take the bets and keep his mouth shut. As he put the money in his pocket, Demetrius asked, "Which fight you betting on?"

I can make the most money on Ali's fight, right?"

"Yeah, there's an extra five percent take on that one," Demetrius answered.

"Then put it all on that one."

"You putting your money on Ali?" Demetrius knew he was supposed to take the money and run. However, he couldn't help but question an action like that. Coach Johnson had been a school teacher and a coach. Demetrius had always thought that the man was smarter than most, but this was just dumb.

"You crazy, boy?" Sam laughed at the thought. "A decade ago I would have bet my entire life savings on ol' Float-Like-A-Butterfly-Sting-Like-A-Bee. But he's all punched out. Ali don't have no business getting in that ring, but since he is, I might as well make enough money to get me and the misses on our way... Put me down for that Trevor Berbick."

Demetrius grinned the whole way home. Coach Johnson wasn't falling for the okie-doke. He wasn't listening to the word that had been put on the street about Ali's conditioning, and about how 'The Greatest' boxer of all times would rise up against this nobody challenger. If everything goes right, then Coach Johnson and his wife would be able to retire in style and in a warmer climate.

As he was rounding the corner to his place, his beeper went off twice, like somebody was trying to get hold of him in a hurry. He glanced at the number. Both calls were from Angel. When he pulled into his driveway and saw Vivian's Ford Explorer, he then figured that Angel was blowing up his beeper because of his dinner guest.

Getting out of the car, Demetrius headed for the door, but Vivian rolled her window down and called him over to her car. "What are you doing out here? Didn't I tell you to wait for me inside?"

Vivian pointed toward the house. "Tell that to the little woman of the house. She told me that I wasn't stepping foot inside that house until she talked to you first."

"Well I'm here now, so let's go eat."

Vivian sucked her teeth, but she climbed out of her SUV and shimmied over to Demetrius. As she locked her arm with his, she asked, "Why we eating at your house anyway? Why can't you take me to a restaurant?"

Vivian had on this floral print dress that hugged her hips and had beads decorating the waistline and the low cut neckline. The three-inch heels she sported only added to the brilliance of the outfit. Another time and another place, Demetrius would have been all over Vivian. He would have proudly made reservations and escorted her to any five-star restaurant her heart desired. But things had changed. And as beautiful as Vivian was, she couldn't take away the heartache he was dealing with over not being able to touch Angel.

He wasn't planning on letting Angel know that her distance was troubling him. She didn't want him… wanted to keep everything about business, then fine. But he wasn't going to act like a monk in his own home not one more day.

"Girl, them restaurants don't have nothing on my cook. Angel's food'll make you slap your mama's mama."

"You telling me that She-Devil's name is Angel?"

"Come on, Angel's not so bad. I forgot to tell her that you were coming for dinner. She takes really good care of my house, and probably didn't want to do anything that might upset me." Demetrius opened the door and shouted for Angel.

But it was DeMarcus who came waddling out of the room. He fell to the ground before he reached Demetrius and crawled the rest of the way. He then climbed into Demetrius' arm while yelling, "Daddy!"

"Daddy?" Vivian said as she stepped inside the house and stared at the little boy in Demetrius' arms. "I thought you didn't have any kids?"

"I don't," He put DeMarcus down just as Angel came into the living room. "DeMarcus is Angel's son. I'm the only man he's been around lately so he's just confused, that's all."

Angel scooped DeMarcus up. "Come back to our room, little boy. You have no business out here with these people."

"He's not bothering us, Angel. Let him stay." Demetrius grabbed for DeMarcus, but she moved the boy out of his reach.

"I wouldn't dream of letting *my* son interfere with your date." As Angel said the word 'date', she cut her eyes at Vivian, and then headed back towards her room.

"What's that supposed to mean?" Demetrius asked as he followed behind Angel, completely ignoring the fact that his date was waiting for him in the living room.

Angel put DeMarcus down in front of the army men that Demetrius brought home the other night. "Don't bother us, Demetrius. Go, go entertain your little girlfriend."

"I didn't say she was my girlfriend, but if that's what you thought, why didn't you let her in the house?"

50

"How was I supposed to know who she was? Who comes to somebody's house dressed like that?"

"What's wrong with the way I'm dressed?" Vivian yelled as she headed to the back of the house where Demetrius and Angel were.

"Nothing… if you're selling it," Angel said while glaring at Vivian as if the woman had stolen from her.

Vivian lunged for Angel, but Demetrius grabbed her arms and moved her back to the front of the house. "Hold up on that, Vivian. Y'all not about to break up my stuff."

"You just gon' let her call me a hooker like that?" Vivian snatched away from him.

"Don't let her get under your skin. Angel was stripping when I met her, so she has no room to talk."

"What!" Vivian was gearing up for a fight now. She slid out of her heels and started taking off her earrings. "She sitting up here a stripper and got the nerve to call somebody else out their name." Vivian tried to get back to Angel's bedroom, but she couldn't get around the immovable force in front of her.

"You not getting ready to fight in my house. Let's just go into the kitchen and get something to eat, and then I'll take you to a movie or something."

"Are you crazy?" Vivian shouted. "I wouldn't eat nothing in this house; and you might want to hire a food taster if you're going to keep eating her food."

Six

Demetrius pulled into the parking lot of a steakhouse. He was about to open Vivian's door so they could go inside, when his beeper went off. It was Coach Johnson. He told Vivian, "Let me answer this before we go inside."

"It's not that she-devil is it?"

"Don't get in my business, Vivian." Demetrius drove to the nearest pay phone and got out of the car without saying another word about it.

He hadn't turned the money in for Coach Johnson's bet yet, and Demetrius was silently hoping the man had come to his senses. He would love nothing more than to give him his money back. Coach answered the phone and Demetrius said, "Did Mrs. Johnson find out about your crazy bet, and threaten to knock your head off if you didn't get the money back?" Demetrius was joking, but never-the-less, if he was right, he'd probably jump for joy.

"No smart mouth, I called to put you in touch with a friend of mine. Danny Green wants to put in a bet on the Frazier fight. And he's got more money than I do, so you might want to hurry over there."

He wanted Coach to take his money back. But if he wasn't doing that, the next best thing was to bring more customers into the fold.

Demetrius smiled. His cut from these fights was going to be huge. He was putting in the hours and it was paying off. "Okay, give me his address and I'll head right there."

When he got back in the car, he told Vivian, "I got to make a run."

"Are you serious? I'm hungry, Demetrius. This isn't right. You asked me out and it's been nothing but one big hassle all night long."

"Alright girl, calm down. There's a McDonald's on the way."

She didn't respond to that until Demetrius actually pulled into a McDonald's and ordered two double cheese burger meals. "This is not for real. Why are you treating me like this?" Vivian screamed at him.

"You said you were hungry. I've got business to take care of and since you can't wait, I pulled in here to get something quick. Now what do you want to drink?"

Rolling her eyes she said, "Nothing, just take me back to my car."

He ordered iced tea with both meals, picked up their food at the to-go window and then kept driving.

"I asked you to take me back to my car."

"I will, Vivian. I just need to make a quick stop. This is about business. So, if you want to be with me, you've got to understand that business comes first." He put the bag in her lap and said, "Just eat your food and give me a minute."

In a huff, she turned her face toward the window and crossed her arms around her chest.

The night was not turning out the way Demetrius had imagined at all. He thought he'd feel better about things if he started dating again. But all these women were high maintenance and more trouble than he had time for. He pulled up to Danny Green's house and cut off the car. "I'll be right back. So, just hold tight, okay?"

"I don't have a choice now do I?" Vivian said as she cut her eyes at Demetrius and then grabbed the McDonald's bag.

His dates normally enjoyed spending time with him. Vivian, however, wasn't enjoying herself at all. Demetrius wished he could feel bad about that. But when Danny Green handed him twenty G's, all guilt went out the door. He would take her to that soul food restaurant up Gettysburg, and let her order a piece of pie or something.

~~~~

Angel didn't understand why she was crying so much. She just knew that she had become so angry that she could barely see straight. She and Demetrius had been getting along so well, that Angel had begun to wonder if he was the guy for her. She had been trying to get her nerve up all week to ask how he felt about her. But she didn't have to ask now.

If bringing that woman home didn't show her just what he thought, then hearing him tell Vivian that she was nothing more than a stripper certainly did. "We're getting out of here, Mar-Mar."

Her son was stretched out on the bed sleep, but she kept talking to him anyway. DeMarcus was all she had in this world; he would never let her down. And she was so tired of being let down by men that she thought she could trust. Her father had been her world and Angel wanted nothing more than to follow in his footsteps, until the day the good reverend got caught cheating on her mother.

After leaving home to get away from all the drama, Angel ran into Frankie, another man she thought she could trust. But he beat her, made her work at his strip club, and was about to pimp her out until Demetrius showed up.

Angel plopped down against the wall, put her head on her knees and balled her eyes out. Demetrius came off as if he was that guy. The one that she could finally trust. But he was no better than her father or Frankie. How could he treat her like that? Angel didn't know what to do. She was yet again stuck. She was once again dealing with a man who had no intentions of doing the right thing.

Just as she was about to lose all hope and wave the white flag, she heard a still small voice say, '*Before I formed you in the womb I knew you; Before you were born I sanctified you; I ordained you a prophet to the nations'*.

*He*r father had read that passage in the Bible to her on numerous occasions. Angel even remembered that the scripture that had somehow been whispered in her ear was in the book of Jeremiah. And there was another part to that scripture that her father used to read to her, but she couldn't remember the rest of it for the life of her.

Demetrius kept a Bible in the top drawer of his dresser. He and his little girlfriend had left the house, because they were afraid that she might have put something in the food… Good. She was glad they didn't want to eat her food.

Angel got off the floor, wiped the tears from her face and went into Demetrius' room to borrow his Bible. She sat on his bed and turned the pages until she reached the first Chapter of Jeremiah. And there it was. After the Lord told Jeremiah that he knew him before he was formed and that he was ordained to be a prophet. Then came the answer from Jeremiah, and it had always been the way she had felt herself…

Then said, I: Ah, Lord God! Behold, I cannot speak, for I am a youth." But the Lord said to me: "Do not say, I am a youth,' For you shall go to all to whom I send you, and whatever I command you, you shall speak.

She had asked her father what the passage meant, and he'd told her that God had something special for her. As Angel put the Bible back in Demetrius' dresser, she was convinced of one thing. She wasn't meant to be here. She was supposed to be doing something special for the Lord. But she had allowed her father's sins to stop her from fulfilling all that God had created her to do.

Her mother was probably worried sick about her. She had only tried to reach out to her mother one time since she'd been gone. By that time her telephone had been disconnected. Life had been miserable in Winston-Salem. Angel had never wanted to return. But the more she thought about the predicament she was in, the more she thought that she just might need her mother.

Maybe if she went home, she could finally figure out why she had been born in the first place. If God had her on His mind before she was even born, then she had to be meant for something much more than what she had become. Right?

She went back to her room and started packing. Angel had about a hundred bucks to her name. If it wasn't enough to get a one way ticket home, she would beg for spare change until she had enough. She called a cab to take her to the Greyhound bus station, and then finished packing. She and DeMarcus waited in the living room for the cab to arrive.

This room had come to mean so much to Angel in the time that she'd spent at Demetrius' home, because this had become their gathering place. After eating dinner, Demetrius would help her with the dishes, because he didn't like for her to be stuck in the kitchen while he and DeMarcus sat watching TV. Then the three of them would retire to the living room for an evening of baseball or whatever TV show happened to be on that night.

She thought their friendship was developing into something more… much more than either of them could have imagined. But with the way Demetrius treated her today, like she was nothing more than the hired help, here to fix meals so he could entertain guests, Angel realized she had only been fooling herself. "What's taking that cab so long?" Angel wiped fresh tears from her face and got up to go look out the window. But before she made it to the window, the doorbell rang.

Without thinking she swung open the door, getting ready to ask the driver to help with her bags so she could get DeMarcus. But the cab driver wasn't on the opposite side of the door looking back at her. It was Mo.

He rubbed his hands together as he said, "Demetrius told me about the lasagna you cooked yesterday. Said it was the best in town."

Angel waved him into the house. "The lasagna's in the fridge. Help yourself."

"Where's Demetrius?"

"Out."

"But he told me to come over here for dinner," Mo Complained.

"He likes telling people to show up over here, whether he's home or not." Angel threw herself back on the sofa and sighed.

"What's all this?" Mo pointed to the bags.

"Nothing. Just my stuff. I'm waiting on a cab."

"Oh, okay." Mo stepped into the kitchen and put in a 911 call to Demetrius' beeper.

The house phone rang in less than a minute. When Mo picked up, Demetrius said, "You're calling from my house, is everything okay with Angel? DeMarcus isn't hurt is he?"

"Angel is packed and waiting on a cab, bro. What you do to this girl, her eyes are all puffy from crying?"

"Mo man, don't let her get in that cab. I'm on my way back."

He stepped back into the living room and asked Angel. "Can you help me heat this lasagna up? I don't know nothing about the kitchen."

Angel gave him a skeptical look. "Who was that on the phone?"

"Demetrius. He said he needs to talk to you before you leave."

"He can shove it. I don't have anything else to say to him."

"Where you plan on going? I thought you didn't have no place to stay."

"I don't have any place here, but I'm going back home to my mom's place. I sure don't want to be where I'm not wanted. That's a fact." And even though it was the last thing Angel wanted to happen in that moment, another tear drifted down her face.

"Whoa." Mo, lifted his hands as he backed up, not sure what to do about the crying woman in front of him. "I don't know what went on here tonight, but Demetrius ain't never said that he didn't want you here."

"Whatever," Angel said as the doorbell rang. "Can you help me with my bags?"

"Yeah, yeah. You sit there and get little man ready. "I'll handle this." He grabbed her bags and opened the front door.

"Did you call for a cab?" the driver asked.

Mo closed the door behind him and followed the driver to the car. The driver opened his trunk so Mo could put the bags inside. But instead of doing that, Mo took two twenties off his stack and handed them to the driver. "Take that for your trouble, my man. I changed my mind about leaving."

"You don't want the ride?" the cabbie looked puzzled.

"No, so just go. Leave right now," Mo urged the man and then headed back to the house as the cabbie got into his car and backed out of the driveway.

Angel opened the door. She had DeMarcus on her hip and his car seat in her hand. The driver was backing out of the driveway. He sped off as she yelled. "Wait! Where are you going?"

Mo walked over to her and admitted, "I told him to leave."

"Why'd you do that? I need to get out of here." It was hard enough to make the decision to go back home and deal with all of the disappointments there. Now Mo had sent the cab away and she would have to convince herself to stay the course.

"Look, I'm sorry for interfering, but you and Demetrius belong together."

"He has a girlfriend, Mo. Demetrius doesn't want me and I just want to go back home." At that moment, Demetrius pulled into the driveway and jumped out of his car.

Vivian got out also. She was yelling at Demetrius, "As long as you stay black, don't you never call me again. Do you hear me, Demetrius? Lose my number." She strutted over to her car and swung open the door.

Angel threw her hands up, went back into the house and slammed the door.

"Good looking out, Man." Demetrius took the bag from Mo as he patted him on the back.

"She's hurt, man. You need to go handle that."

Vivian rolled her window down and kept on yelling at him. "To think that you'd rather have a stripper than somebody like me. That just goes to show that you don't have good sense... wouldn't nobody give you the time of day if you weren't Don Shepherd's boy."

Trying to ignore Vivian he told Mo. "Coach Johnson's friend just gave me a twenty thousand dollar bet. Since Coach talked to you first, I figure it's only right that you and I split the earnings from both those bets."

"Sounds good to me," Mo said just as Vivian threw a shoe at Demetrius' head. "You want me to handle that?"

Demetrius ducked and said, "Please get that girl off my property."

Vivian threw the other shoe, but Mo caught it as Demetrius opened the door and went inside. He put her bags on the floor and then walked towards her. "What are you doing? Where you trying to go?"

Tears were rolling down Angel's face as she said, "I need to go home. My parents have never even seen my son."

He kept walking until he was standing right in front of her. "I don't want to stop you from seeing your parents. But why you got to leave like this?"

"Why do you care? I'm nothing but a stripper, remember?"

"I didn't say you were *nothing* but a stripper. I just said that you used to be a stripper, that's all."

Angel turned her back to him. "How could you tell that girl something like that? What I used to do is none of your girlfriend's business."

"You're right, and I was wrong for that."

Angel shook her head as she walked back to her bedroom and closed the door.

Demetrius followed, he tried the door but it was locked. "Open up Angel. We need to talk about this." She didn't respond, so he said,

"Vivian isn't my girlfriend, okay. I used to hang out with her, but I haven't seen her since you moved in."

"Then why'd you invite her to dinner?" She screamed at him from behind the door.

"I ran into her at the club last night and… and," He didn't know what to do other than tell it like it is. "I need to get you off my mind, okay. You were acting like you wanted nothing from me, so I thought I should start seeing someone so I wouldn't try to push up on you."

She opened the door and peaked her head out. "You wanted to get with me?"

"That's all I've been thinking about, girl. But you all like 'don't-touch-me'. So, I thought I should move on."

And with that admission from Demetrius, all thoughts of moving on and going home to discover what God had her on earth to do, completely left her mind. Demetrius wanted her around, and that was all that mattered.

Seven

On December the third, the fight between Joe Frazier and hulking Floyd "Jumbo" Cummings got under way. The fight took place in Chicago, Illinois and the gang was in attendance. Demetrius, Joe-Joe and Stan were seated in the third row, down on the floor like celebrities. His dad had said he would meet them there. Demetrius assumed that Al was late getting in town and Don was waiting on him.

Joe-Joe nudged him and Demetrius turned to see his father strutting down the middle aisle with a long haired, dark skinned beauty on his arm. Don and the woman both had on floor length fur coats; his father's was black with hints of grey around the collar. The coat the woman wore was snow white, contrasting beautifully with her skin. His daddy was showing off tonight.

Demetrius was slightly annoyed by this because he had asked for an extra ticket so that he could bring Angel to the fight. But he'd been told that this was a business trip, no distractions allowed. Angel had given him the cold shoulder after he told her he would be spending the weekend in Chicago. Sometimes he didn't understand that girl at all, but that didn't stop him from longing to be near her.

Don and his lady sat in the second row directly in front of Demetrius. He leaned over and asked his daddy, "Where's Al, I thought he was coming to the fight?"

"He's holding things down at home. We'll see him when we get back."

Demetrius leaned back in his seat wondering who this woman was and why Al suddenly decided not to attend the fight. But he didn't have much time to dwell on it because the bell rang. Smokin' Joe Frazier and Floyd "Jumbo" Cummings entered the ring. This was the first time anyone had seen Joe Frazier in the ring since George Foreman pummeled him over five years ago. But this fight was going to be Joe's coming out party. Once he destroyed this opponent, he wasn't going to stop until he got his shot at the WBA heavyweight champion, Mike Weaver.

Those were Joe's plans. But Floyd "Jumbo" Cummings was a body-building bruiser, who'd taken up boxing in prison after being convicted of murder. And he wasn't about to give any mercy to the aging Frazier, who's reactions and timing were glaringly off.

In the opening round Frazier stepped into punch after punch. It wasn't hard for the audience to see and believe that Frazier's glory days were long gone. No one wanted to see the aging fighter go down like this… no one, except Don Shepherd, who had millions riding on Frazier's demise. He glanced back at his boys and smiled.

Demetrius leaned forward to say something to his dad, but that's when he noticed that Don had a hand on the woman's thigh. He nudged Joe-Joe and asked, "Who's the new squeeze?"

Joe-Joe smirked. He leaned closer to Demetrius and whispered in his ear. "That's Lisa Wilson. Leo's wife."

Demetrius nearly fell out of his chair. His father had said that splitting the proceeds from these fights with Leo would benefit the man's family. But Demetrius was pretty sure that Leo wouldn't think that sleeping with his wife was any sort of benefit that he signed up for. His dad was a snake and Demetrius again longed for the day that he was on his own and doing things his way.

As the second round began, Demetrius turned his attention back to the ring. Frazier's left hook landed just right and the crowd went wild. Smokin' Joe Frazier was back in business. Demetrius leaned back in his seat and enjoyed the show. Maybe this would be the night that Don Shepherd got what was coming to him. Because Joe was showing some brilliance throughout the rounds. His best punch of the night came in the fifth round, which sparked hope in the audience yet again. But by the ninth round Cummings appeared to be in control.

Frazier's blood soaked mouth hung open as Cummings kept drilling on him. Joe was in trouble, and even he knew it as he almost hit the canvas in the last round. But managed to hang in there to get a draw decision after the tenth round.

Demetrius expected to see nothing but pure joy on his father's face. But the man appeared troubled. The fight was a draw, so nobody wins and they wouldn't have to shell out any money. But then Demetrius remembered that two men had bet on a draw. One of them was his customer, Danny Green who had been introduced to him by Mr. Johnson. The old man had twenty thousand to burn. So, he put it all on the Frazier fight… saying that he knew for a fact that Smokin' Joe had enough left in him to go the distance, but not enough to win. And as long as he was left standing by the end of the fight, the judges would call it a draw.

The other guy had been one of Stan's customers. That man put five thousand on the fight. So, Demetrius understood why his father suddenly looked like he had lost everything. Because most of their bets had been ten, twenty or a hundred dollars. Hood life didn't afford many black men the luxury of sitting on tens of thousands of dollars. But a few of them had it, because they had been diligent savers, and now they were willing to risk it all for a chance at big money.

Demetrius put a hand on his father's shoulder and said, "Don't worry about it, Dad. You can afford it. Those two draw bets are nothing compared to all the money we just took in."

Don snatched away from his son. "You don't know what I can and can't afford. Just keep your mouth shut."

Demetrius got up and stormed out of the arena. He didn't need to be in his father's presence another second. He could kick rocks for all Demetrius cared. The rest of the gang was planning to hang out in Chicago for the weekend and go clubbing to celebrate. But with the way his father was acting, Demetrius didn't want to be anywhere around the man. He got in his car and headed back home to Dayton.

~~~~

Angel couldn't stop smiling when she heard Demetrius' car pull into the driveway at around three that morning. That meant he wasn't spending the weekend in Chicago with his father, getting into Lord knows what kind of trouble. Honestly, when Demetrius told her he was going to Chicago for the entire weekend with his dad, she thought he was probably taking Vivian or some other woman with him.

She felt a little guilty for the not even saying goodbye to him when he left on the trip. So she got up extra early that morning, started frying bacon and flipping pancakes. She even scrambled a few eggs for him, just the way he liked them.

By seven thirty that morning Demetrius came out of his room, rubbing his tired eyes and asking, "What smells so good?"

"Your eggs are almost done, and I've got pancakes and some of that thick cut bacon that you like so much."

"Is it my birthday and somebody forgot to tell me?"

Angel could admit that she hadn't been doing all that much cooking since Demetrius brought that woman into the house a few weeks back, but she hadn't let him starve or nothing. So, he could quit it. "Don't act like I'm not on my job around here."

"All I know is I've been eating a lot of baloney sandwiches lately."

"Sorry about that," Angel mumbled as she flipped her last pancake.

"What… what was that?" He put his hand to his ear as if he was hard of hearing.

She held the skillet filled with eggs over the trash can. "I said… if you don't sit down and eat, I'm going to throw this food in the trash."

Demetrius grabbed a plate out of the cabinet and handed it to her. "Girl, as hungry as I am I would climb in that trash can and get my breakfast."

Laughing at him, she said, "Boy, you silly. Sit down while I fix your plate."

Demetrius turned the television that was on the kitchen counter to the news, and then sat down and eagerly awaited his breakfast.

"Did you enjoy the fight?" Angel asked as she sat his plate along with the syrup in front of him.

While pouring the syrup on his pancakes, Demetrius said, "I thought it was going to be a fun time. But I didn't enjoy seeing Frazier like that. The man had been one of my childhood heroes; I didn't think nobody could out do Joe Frazier. Even when he lost to

Ali, I still felt like he put up a good fight. But, that wasn't the same fighter in the ring last night."

"He probably should have stayed retired," Angel said as she moved away from the table.

"Sit down and eat with me this morning," Demetrius urged.

"I'm coming, just grabbing a plate for myself."

Demetrius smiled at the thought of Angel eating breakfast with him. But as she sat down a fire was blazing on the television and the newscaster was saying, "This is the home of Professor Daniel Green and his wife Olivia. Many of you will remember that Olivia Green was a member of the city council for over a decade in the seventies. She retired last year."

The reporter pointed at the house as he continued, "The fire was put out a few hours ago, and it saddens this reporter to inform our viewers that the Green family did not survive. Their bodies were found inside."

Demetrius had been eating his pancakes, but as the reporter finished detailing the situation, he lost his appetite.

"What's wrong?" Angel asked as his fork hit his plate.

"I know him." Demetrius pointed at the burning house. "I was at his house a few weeks ago." He didn't bother to inform Angel that Danny Green had placed a twenty thousand dollar bet with him. And that if he had lived through the night, he would be collecting about two hundred thou. But with Mr. Green dead, his father was now off the hook.

Eight

Don Shepherd was back in town and it was time for Demetrius to collect his earning from the fight. He wanted to ask his father if he had heard about the fire at Professor Green's house, but something told him that he didn't want the answer to that question. Instead, he asked, "Did you have fun with Leo's wife this weekend?"

"As a matter-of-fact, I did," Don told his son with a silly grin on his face.

Demetrius sat down in front of his father's desk. He shook his head. "Aren't you worried about what Leo's going to do about you fooling around with his wife all out in the open like that?"

Don stood and walked around his desk. He sat on the edge of it while telling his son, "Leo is done in this town. He's going to be locked up until he's a very old man. There's nothing he can do to me. Because if his boys want to keep living good and eating good, they'll be joining our team." Shrugging he added, "Half of 'em have already called me."

"So just like that, you become kingpin around here... and to the king, goes the queen, huh?"

"You better know it." Don patted his son on the back and then walked over to the wall safe. He opened it and took out two stacks. He put the money in Demetrius' lap. "Go buy yourself another car or something. Take that stripper out and do up the town… whatever you want. You earned it."

Demetrius had seen first-hand how much it had hurt Angel when he'd told Vivian that she had been a stripper. Now he understood why she'd become so angry, because he didn't like the way those words fell off his father's lips. "She's not a stripper. Angel is good people."

"You watch yourself, boy. Don't go get your nose opened by some chick that just might leave you as fast as she left Frankie Day. In our business you need a woman who's going to be down for you."

"I'm not worried about Angel. You're the one who needs to sleep with one eye open… over there with Leo's woman."

Don harrumphed as he tugged on the belt of his pants. "Your old man got this, believe that. I ain't never met a woman I couldn't tame."

Before Demetrius could respond to that, Al strutted in swinging his keys with one hand while the other was stuffed in his pocket. He looked relaxed, liked he'd enjoyed his weekend. "What up, black people?"

"You know what it is," Don responded as he and Al fist bumped.

"Hey stranger, long time no see," Demetrius said as he studied Al. "Why didn't you go to the fight?"

Al shrugged the question off. "Had too much to do around here to be hanging out in Chicago."

"You didn't miss much. I doubt if Frazier will ever get in the ring again." Demetrius shook his head. "Saddest thing I've ever seen."

"That's because you haven't been to the Ali fight yet." Al put his fists up and boxed around the room. He then turned back to Demetrius and said, "Ali is about to get stung."

"And then we are going to make another boat load of money," Don said as he went back to the safe, pulled out a stash and handed it to Al.

"Now, get on back out there and keep selling them Ali dreams," Don said. "We've got less than seven days before we hear the ring of that bell."

"And Ali goes down," Al laughed.

"Keep that to yourself while you're out there taking bets. Ali is still the greatest as far as we're concerned."

Demetrius got up and headed for the door along with Al. But Don stopped them.

"Wait a minute, Demetrius. I don't want any of our customers getting cute this week and making 'draw' bets. It's either Ali wins or he loses, that's it."

~~~~~

Demetrius knew that he should have been out there taking bets and collecting numbers, but he had a bundle of cash and was itching to spend some of it. So, he called Angel and told her to be dressed and ready to go by the time he got to the house.

The car seat was still in the back of his SUV since their last trip to the grocery store. Angel came out the door carrying her purse, the baby bag and the baby. Demetrius rushed to her side and grabbed DeMarcus out of her arm. He strapped him into the car seat and then got back into the driver's seat.

"Thank you," Angel said while looking at Demetrius as if the single act of strapping her son into a car seat had caused her to see him in a different light.

"Looked like you could use some help." Demetrius pointed at DeMarcus. "And little man back there is picking up weight."

"I haven't been out shaking my money maker and leaving it to someone else to feed him. DeMarcus has been getting three, sometimes four meals a day."

Demetrius eyed DeMarcus as he said, "Boy, I'm gon' put a lock on them cabinets. Don't nobody eat more than three meals a day unless he has a job."

Angel shoved at Demetrius shoulder. "Leave him alone. He's a growing baby."

"Well he can eat whatever he wants today. And I'm going to buy him a bunch of toys too," Demetrius told her.

"What's got you in the mood to splurge?"

"I'm flush baby… just got paid," he told her as they pulled out of the driveway and headed to the mall.

Angel was grinning from ear to ear as she picked out toys and new shoes for DeMarcus. But when Demetrius turned to her and said, "Okay, DeMarcus is all squared away. Now, what does his mama want?"

She shook her head, "I don't want anything, Demetrius. You've been so good to me already that I can't take anything else from you."

Demetrius wanted to pull Angel into Macy's and buy her everything that he thought would look good on her. But he could see in her eyes that she still didn't trust him. Maybe she thought that if she took too much from him, that one day he would put her on the stroll like Frankie tried to do… heck, like his own father did to his mother.

So he didn't fight the issue. He simply said, "Can I at least take you to dinner?"

"As much as I cook for you… boy, you better take me to dinner."

Putting her arm in his, he said, "Okay girl, just tell me where you want to go, and I will make sure you get there."

"I've got a taste for seafood. How about Red Lobster?"

"Let's hit it and get it." Demetrius took DeMarcus out of Angel's arm as they headed to the car. He locked him back in his car seat and then they headed to Red Lobster.

Angel ordered shrimp and a baked potato with chicken fingers for DeMarcus. Demetrius ordered lobster. When the plates arrived, Angel told him, "I wanted to order lobster, but it cost too much."

Demetrius was dumbfounded. He'd told her to order whatever she wanted and still she had picked shrimp instead of the lobster. Now she was looking like she wanted to grab his plate and make a run for it. Demetrius lifted a hand, getting the attention of the waitress. When the waitress came back to the table he said, "Can you bring another lobster fest and put her shrimp in a to-go box."

"You didn't have to do that," Angel told him when the waitress left the table with her plate.

"You should have ordered what you wanted in the first place." Demetrius shook his head. "I don't know what I'm going to do with you. One day you'll realize that you're worth a lot more than you think."

"I'm not concerned about what I'm worth. I'm more worried about what certain things might cost me in the end."

Putting his fork down, Demetrius was clearly offended. "I don't know how many times I have to tell you that I am not Frankie. I'm not looking for anything more than what you want to give."

"That's what you say now. But what happens once I let my guard down?"

He wanted to tell her that his guard was already down, because he had fallen for her. Angel was the one for him, and Demetrius didn't care what anybody else had to say about it. But if she didn't know by now that she could trust him, how could he even begin to share his heart with her?

"Out spending your earnings from the Frazier fight I see."

Demetrius was caught off guard as he looked up to see Coach Johnson. He smiled at first but then he noticed the angry expression on the man's face. "I saw the news, I'm sorry about Mr. Green."

Sam Johnson put his hands on the table and leaned so close to Demetrius that they were almost nose to nose. "You can tell your daddy that I got my gun locked and loaded."

"What are you talking about? You don't have anything to fear from us." Demetrius was shocked by the way his former coach was acting. They had never had any bad blood.

"That fire at Danny's house was no accident. Same old Don Shepherd... don't want to pay his debts. But I better get my money after that Ali fight; or I'm going to have a bullet for the one that tries to take me out." With that said, Johnson stalked off.

"What was that about," Angel asked as she pulled DeMarcus out of his high chair and sat him in her lap.

"Let's just eat our dinner. I don't want to talk about this right now." Demetrius turned his head and watched his former coach open the door and walk out of the restaurant. The man had been good to him since the time he was a child playing in little league baseball. Coach Johnson had trusted him with his life savings, and now the man thought that he would rather kill him, than pay if he won his bet. Many times as Demetrius was growing up, he had wished that Coach Johnson had been his dad, because at least Coach had been at all of his games. And had believed in his future. Don Shepherd hadn't even attended his final game. The one Demetrius had broken his ankle in... he'd been too busy in the streets.

Coach Johnson had nothing to fear from him, and he would make sure that no one else did anything to him before he could get his wife to the South just as he'd been planning.

Nine

"Why is it that so many people think we had something to do with Professor Green's death?" Demetrius had put off saying anything to his father for several days, but Coach's words kept eating at him. Then customers started telling him that they didn't want to put their twenty dollar bet in because they heard Don Shepherd doesn't like to pay up. The gang was getting ready to leave for the Bahamas the next day for the Ali fight, and Demetrius didn't want to leave town without getting to the bottom of this.

"Who are these people?" Don snarled.

"Haven't you noticed that I haven't had as many bets this week?"

"Yeah, but I thought you was out spending your money instead of doing your job this week."

"I've been on my job," Demetrius defended himself. "But everywhere I go, someone is telling me that they don't want to place a bet, because they don't want to end up like Professor Green."

"That's just ridiculous. How many house fires do they think can be set in this town without the police asking questions?"

Demetrius just came out with it. "So, are you saying that you didn't do it, or that you wouldn't burn down another house in order to kill someone?"

Don stared at his son for a long moment. When he finally spoke his voice was calm. "Wasn't I in Chicago when Danny's house burned down? If the people are mad because I didn't try to find a family member to give Danny's winnings to, that's one thing... but don't accuse me of murder when I wasn't even in town."

That was true. Demetrius could verify that his father had been in Chicago. At least, he'd been there up until the time Demetrius left. From the timeline given by the newscaster Demetrius had been home, sleeping in his own bed when the fire started at Professor Green's house. So, if he had made it back to Dayton before the fire started, then his father could have done the same. But if Don Shepherd had come back to Dayton the same night of the fire, then why would he have gone back to Chicago? Because from what he knew, Don, Joe-Joe and Stan partied hard in Chicago that weekend.

He shook the doubt off. No, his father was not in Dayton at the time the fire had been set. And his dad was probably right about people having sour grapes because Don wasn't about to give Professor Green's winnings to a family member. It wasn't like they were some legitimate business that could be taken to court.

"You're right, Dad. People around here just mad because they didn't have enough money to make the kind of bet Professor Green made."

"Exactly."

Demetrius stood. "I'm going home to pack. Are you bringing Leo's wife again?"

"What can I say," Don popped his collar. "The lady can't keep her hands off of me."

"Is anybody else bringing a date to this fight?"

"Stan's bringing his old lady." Don laughed as he added, "Joe-Joe is trying to find a lady so he won't be the odd man out."

"Oh, but you don't care if I'm the odd man out. What if I wanted to bring a date? Where's my extra ticket?"

"Don't get your nose out of joint. Al isn't going to make the trip, so I have an extra ticket."

"But I thought he was so excited about seeing this fight. Especially since he thinks it's going to be Ali's last fight?"

Don shrugged, "Changed his mind, I guess."

Sticking his hand out, Demetrius said, "Give me the ticket. Angel would love to go to this fight."

"Boy, you done lost your mind if you think I'm giving you this ticket so you can treat that girl to a Bahamas vacation. Vivian is the girl for you. Why don't you call her up and see if she wants go?"

"Vivian threw a shoe at my head."

"Vivian is cool people. Me and her daddy go way back. That girl will make you a good wife. That's why I've been pushing you towards Vivian for years. But what did you do... you go and pull that little stripper out of an alley and try to make her a house wife.

Demetrius' body trembled from the rage he felt inside. How dare Don act as if Angel wasn't good enough for them. "What has Angel done that makes you dislike her so much? Okay, she was a stripper... but you used to be a pimp. How can you judge her?"

Smirking, Don said, "Being a stripper makes her my kind of people. It's something about her that I don't trust. She don't know her place." Don shook his head as his lip twisted in disgust. "I can't trust her to be down when you might need her to be, so I don't want her anywhere near me."

"You think she's not down just because she wouldn't turn a trick for Frankie Day?" Demetrius' nostrils were flaring. He was so angry he could hardly see straight. "Every woman on these streets isn't like Ma..." Demetrius clamped his mouth shut. He couldn't say the words out loud. He wouldn't discuss what his mother had been, not to the man who had done it to her in the first place. Demetrius was done talking.

Demetrius went to his car, took his ticket for the Ali fight out of his glove compartment and then stormed back into his father's office. He threw the ticket on his desk. "You can have my ticket, because I'm not interested in being down for Don Shepherd either. So, I guess that makes me a liability too, huh?"

Don took the ticket in his hand, he studied his son as he asked, "Does this mean that you don't want to get paid either?"

"I earned my paper. I got up early and stayed out on them streets late taking bets, so yeah, I want what's mine. And don't think you can just set a fire to get out of paying me."

Don's hand hit the desk hard. "There aren't too many men still living who can boast about talking to me the way you just did. Being in the family has its privileges, but don't overstep yourself, son." He opened his desk drawer and pulled out the extra ticket. "Here, bring whoever you want."

"I just told you that I don't want to go."

Don stood up, leaning forward, "And I'm telling you that I don't want you in town this weekend. You will be with me in the Bahamas, got it?"

Demetrius didn't reach for the tickets. He and his father just kept staring at each other as if in a contest to see who would break first.

Don finally said, "It's like this, Demetrius. I don't want anyone to be able to get at you while I'm all the way in the Bahamas. We are going to have a ton of angry customers when this fight ends. I need to know that you're safe." He pushed the tickets toward his son.

Demetrius took them this time, but he left without saying another word to his father. He just didn't understand how Don Shepherd could judge anybody, when he had been a pimp, a loan shark, numbers runner and now they were getting into the dope game. Sure, his father had legitimate businesses like a car wash and a neighborhood drive-thru. But they were only fronts for the other illegal activity.

Still steaming as he drove home, Demetrius wondered if his dad had said anything to Stan or Joe-Joe about the women they were bringing to the fight. But as he was thinking that over, another thought struck him… Al wasn't going to the Bahamas.

Al hadn't gone to Chicago for the Frazier fight either. So, Al had been in town when Professor Green's house had caught on fire. Demetrius didn't want to believe it, but the more he thought about it, the more it all made sense.

As he pulled into his driveway, Demetrius turned off the engine but didn't get out of the car. He was too busy thinking… His dad had been angry when the fight ended with a draw, he'd even snapped at him. Demetrius had expected his father to still be in a bad mood when he'd come home from Chicago, because it would now be time to pay up. But Don had been jovial about the matter. When Demetrius and Al had shown up to collect their earnings, Don had told them that Stan and Joe-Joe were making the rounds paying the winners from the Frazier fight. He had even said, paying up quickly ensured that most of them would put money on the Ali fight.

Paying a hundred dollars to the person who placed a ten dollar bet, was a whole lot easier than paying two hundred thou to the man who'd placed a twenty thousand dollar bet. But once that fire had been set, Don's two hundred thousand dollar problem had been solved.

Beating down a man who owed money and wasn't trying to pay it back was one thing; but killing a man and his wife to get out of paying a debt, was way past wrong as far as Demetrius was concerned. This wasn't the business he wanted to be in. All of his young life he'd dreamed of being a hitter. Demetrius could swing that bat like nobody's business.

But that was back in the day. Now he was a thug who beat up people and took bets for a living. If his mother could see him now, Demetrius knew one thing for sure, she would be heart broken. His father could talk all his a-woman-has-to-be-down-for-her-man stuff that he wanted, but the real truth was, his mother never wanted him to become anything like her husband.

Demetrius hit the steering wheel with his fist, as he screamed out, "How could you get pregnant by a man like him? How could you leave me with him?" He wished his mother could have answered those questions, but that would never happen and he had one person to thank for that.

"Hey, are you going to sit in that car all night or what?" Angel called out to him as she opened the front door.

Demetrius glanced at his watch. He'd been sitting in his car for over an hour. Still trying to come to grips with the fact that his father was a cold blooded killer, just as Coach Johnson had said. But there was nothing he could do about his father, so he decided to go into the house and make Angel's day. "I'm coming."

The moment he walked in, he showed her the tickets.

Angel stepped back as she looked at them. Then she asked as sadness crept into her eyes, "You're taking someone to the Ali fight?"

"Oh yeah, I'm taking someone alright. And we are going to have a good time in the Bahamas."

Folding her arms across her chest, she asked, "Are your bags packed already, or am I supposed to do that?"

Demetrius had been grinning as he twirled the tickets around. But he stopped as he looked into Angel's eyes. He realized that Angel thought he would show her tickets to a fight even though he planned to take someone else. Frankie must have done a real number on her. He wished she'd never met that man, but Demetrius vowed right then and there to spend the rest of his life making up for what that low-life had done.

"No, I don't want you to pack my bags. You won't have time. You need to get in your room and pack a bag for you and DeMarcus because we are going to the Bahamas together, baby."

"What!" she screamed as she started jumping around the room.

"You heard me. The only thing I need to do now is get you a plane ticket because I think DeMarcus should be able to sit on your lap."

Without thinking, Angel jumped into Demetrius' arms and kissed him. "I love you, Demetrius." Her eyes got big as those words rolled out of her mouth. She stepped away from him and tried to clarify. "I... I mean, I love this. What we are about to do... the trip. Thank you." She then scurried off to her room without looking back.

Demetrius watched her go, wanting desperately to pull her back and make her face the fact that what they were feeling was real and it was good and wasn't nothing ever going to come between them. But he doubted that she would hear him.

~~~~

Demetrius hadn't been able to book Angel on the same flight he and his father were on because it was full. So, he cancelled his ticket and booked both of them on a flight scheduled to leave out three hours later. He'd also checked with the airline to verify that he didn't need an extra ticket for DeMarcus. And they'd confirmed that since the child was under two years old, he could just sit in Angel's lap.

He and Angel spent the rest of the night talking about their upcoming trip. She was all smiles and totally jubilant, because she'd never dreamed that she would be able to go anywhere other than back home to North Carolina. And she told Demetrius just that.

He asked, "You've mentioned going back home a few times. Is it really that important to you?"

Angel nodded. "I don't really care to see my father, butI owe my mom a serious apology. I blamed her for the break-up and wouldn't listen to reason. I became a rebellious child and really let her down. Now I have a son and she doesn't even know anything about him."

Demetrius wasn't so keen on his father these days either, so he didn't bother to ask why she didn't want to see her father. Instead he asked, "Why don't you just call your mother?"

"I tried about a year ago, right before Frankie made me earn my living by stripping. But her phone had been disconnected."

"What about your father? Do you have a telephone number for him?"

"I'm not trying to call him. One day I'll just go home and find my mother. I still know how to get back to the house we moved into after the divorce." Angel smiled down at DeMarcus as he lay on the sofa sleeping. "She'll be so happy to see her grandson."

Demetrius decided right then and there that he would take her down South to find her mother. Maybe they'd even spend a few weeks in North Carolina. He certainly needed some time and space away from his father. Once he collected his money, he would drive Angel down South. He'd let her in on the plan later this weekend. Right now he wanted to discuss another matter.

"You do understand that you and I will be in the same hotel room when we get to the Bahamas, right?"

"What's that supposed to mean?" Angel looked at him as if waiting for the other shoe to drop.

"It don't mean nothing, except that I want you to be my woman... do you understand what I'm telling you, Angel? I want us to be together?"

She stared at him as she pulled at her lip. Then she asked, "What about Vivian? What about that girl who called the house the other day?"

"I don't want nobody but you. Can you get that through your thick skull already?" He pulled her close to him, this time he kissed her. It was a hungry, throw caution to the wind kind of kiss that left them gasping for air. When he was able to speak again, he said, "I love you, girl. I don't know how it happened or why it happened, but I'm not fighting it."

"I can't fight it anymore either, Demetrius. You're a good man and," tears were in her eyes as she said, "I love you."

"Then let's do the dang thang then."

Angel nodded. Where else could she go? As far as Angel was concerned, this was Demetrius' world and she wanted nothing more than to discover what he was going to do with it.

Ten

That morning was the first time Demetrius woke and didn't want to hurriedly climb out of bed. Because Angel was lying next to him, and all was right with his world. But then the doorbell rang, and rang, and rang.

Demetrius got out of bed, put on a robe and headed for the door. The person on the other end was now pounding on the door. "Hold up. I'm on my way." He looked out the peep hole and saw that it was Al.

Demetrius swung the door open and yelled, "What is wrong with you? Why you over hear banging on my door like the police?"

"I got orders to drive you to the airport this morning?"

Rubbing the sleep from his eyes, Demetrius said, "I can drive myself."

Al just shook his head. "Can't let you do that. Don wants you to have a personal escort to the airport."

"What's his deal? Why does he want me out of this city so bad this weekend?"

"I'm just the chauffeur."

"Well you came at the wrong time because I cancelled my earlier flight so that I could fly over there with Angel."

Al snickered. "That girl has got you turning flips and cartwheels, huh?"

"Whatever."

Al pointed a finger in his face. "And you better watch yourself. Don wasn't happy about the way you spoke to him just because he was trying to school you."

"What's he going to do, kill me?" As the words left his mouth, Demetrius began wondering if his father had in fact sent his enforcer over here to smoke him. His gun was in the bedroom, so if Al made a move, Demetrius wouldn't be able to do anything about it.

"He's your father, kid. He's not going to kill you... but that don't mean he won't fire you... make you find your own way in this big ol' cruel world. So, keep your cool and do as he says."

"Look, my flight doesn't leave until noon. So, go back home and get some sleep. I'm a big boy, I'll get to the airport on my own."

"I'll be back at ten. Y'all need to be dressed and ready to go at that time," Al told him as he walked back to his car.

Demetrius closed the door and then sat down on the sofa as he tried to figure out what his father had up his sleeve. Since Demetrius had already figured out that Al must have been the one who killed Professor Green and his wife, Demetrius could only think of one reason why Don didn't want him in town this weekend... they were planning to kill again.

Demetrius sat on the sofa, trying to figure this out. Who did they plan to kill? And why were they working so hard to get him out of the way. Demetrius figured he must know the target. It had to be someone that Demetrius wouldn't want to see dead. There were a few people Demetrius could put in that category, but he'd only took a ten thousand dollar bet from one of them.

His eyes shut tight from the pain of that thought. He wished he had never accepted that bet from Coach Johnson. The man didn't deserve to be caught in his father's crosshairs. He didn't deserve to die simply because Don Shepherd was too greedy to pay out his big debts.

Putting his head in his hands, Demetrius was mired in guilt and didn't know what to do. If his father was going to kill Coach, then Demetrius wouldn't be able to stop him. No matter how upset he'd been with his father lately, Demetrius couldn't turn against him. That would go against everything he'd been taught all his life.

But Coach was a good man, he didn't deserve to die, and Demetrius just couldn't get on that plane to the Bahamas and act as if he didn't know what was going on.

He was tossing an idea around in his mind as he went to his bedroom to wake Angel up.

"Good morning." She smiled at him as if the very sight of him brightened her day.

"Good morning to you too." He bent down and kissed her on her soft, ample lips. "I've got some bad news."

"What's wrong?"

He ran his hand up her arm. "We can't go to the Bahamas this weekend."

Angel's eyes widened in horror. She sat up in bed, pulling the blanket tightly against her naked flesh. "You tricked me," she screamed at him. "You made me think that I was special to you, just so you could get me in bed. And now you're going to take some other woman to the Bahamas."

This was getting old real fast. "For the last time… I am not that dude. I'm not going to use and abuse you."

86

She wasn't having it. "I don't care what you say, Demetrius. If you go to the Bahamas without us, Mar-Mar and I are getting on the Greyhound and I'm going home to my mother."

Looking at her as if she was a genius, he said, "That's actually not a bad idea."

"What!" Angel swung on him. But Demetrius ducked and then grabbed her arms.

"Listen to me girl. I'm not going to the Bahamas either. So, stop acting crazy."

"You done had your way with me and now you want me to go home. But you don't want me to go off on you... I think you're the one who's acting crazy."

"It's not like that, Angel. Stop tripping and get dressed. Because I'm going to drive you to see your mother this weekend."

Angel did as she was asked. Then went into the living room and sat down on the sofa with Demetrius. "Did you mean what you said? You're going to take me to my mother's place?"

He nodded. "I think it's the perfect cover for us."

"Cover for what? What's going on?"

"Do you remember the man who accused my father of killing his friend?"

"The man who came to our table at Red Lobster?"

"That's him. His name is Sam Johnson. And he is one of the reasons why I love baseball so much. He used to be my coach. He had been the first person to run out on the field to check on me after I broke my ankle. I always liked Coach and when I was younger I used to wish that he was my father."

Angel didn't say anything, she just kept listening.

"I didn't want to believe that my father had killed Professor Green, so when Coach said it, I kind of blew it off. But the truth of the matter is… I think Coach was right."

"Why?" Angel asked.

"Most of the bets we took in for the Frazier and Ali fight were for small amounts. If we had to pay out money on one of those bets it wouldn't be a big deal. But Professor Green put a twenty thousand dollar bet on the Frazier fight. He bet it would end in a draw. Since he was right, my father owed him big money and he didn't want to pay up."

"But I saw how much money you came home with after that Frazier fight. If your father could pay you all that money, why didn't he just settle up with Professor Green?"

"Because he needs the earnings from these fights to be a real player in a new business venture."

"And he'd kill a man for that?"

"I think so," Demetrius said, but he wasn't finished. "Coach Johnson put a ten thousand dollar bet in with me for the Ali fight. He wants to use his winnings to move his wife to the South. But I think my father plans to kill him this weekend."

"Oh my God. That's awful," Angel said.

Demetrius was trusting Angel with information that he shouldn't have shared with anyone. He only prayed that she was about to prove his father wrong and be down for him and not turn a knife in his back. "I can't let my father kill Coach. But I need your help."

"What do you need me to do?"

"Al will be back here in about two hours. He's coming to take us to the airport, because my father wants to make sure that I am out of town this weekend."

"But I thought you said that you weren't going to the Bahamas?"

"I'm not, but you've got to trust me, Angel."

She hesitated for a moment, but only a moment and then said, "I trust you, Demetrius. Just tell me what you want me to do."

"When Al gets here, I'm going to tell him that you couldn't find a babysitter for DeMarcus so you won't be going to the Bahamas after all. I want you to go off on me. Say something like… if I leave then you won't be here when I get back. Like you told me earlier."

Demetrius went to his bedroom and then came back with a stack of cash. He handed it to Angel as he continued, "When I leave with Al. I want you to put your bag in my SUV and go to Coach Johnson's house. Give him this money and then tell him to come with you."

"How much money is this?"

"It's ten thousand dollars. I earned twenty thousand on the Frazier fight, so I'm just giving him his money back."

"And you trust me with this money?"

He looked at her, then squeezed her hand. "I do, Angel. I trust your heart."

"What if Coach Johnson won't come with me?"

"Do whatever you have to do to convince him that he is not safe in this town anymore. Please Angel. You will have to get him to leave with you, because I can't go to his house. He'd never trust me. I'm Don Shepherd's son, remember?"

"Okay, once we leave, then what?"

She and Demetrius sat there for another hour making plans. Then the doorbell rang. Demetrius got up and headed to the door. As he walked he started yelling at Angel. "I don't know what you're mad at me for. It's not my fault that you got this kid and no body to watch him."

He opened the door and Al walked in. "Y'all ready?"

Angel angrily folded her arms across her chest and rolled her eyes as Demetrius said, "I am. But Angel can't find a babysitter. Looks like I've got an extra ticket."

Al's mouth hung open as he looked from Angel to Demetrius. "Are you telling me that you done rearranged everything for this girl, and she couldn't even get off her duff and find a babysitter?"

"Like I said, I've got an extra ticket." Demetrius then looked at Al as if an idea struck him. "Why don't you go with me?"

"Wish I could kid, but I've got important business to take care of this weekend," Al told him.

"What's so important? We've collected all the bets we're going to get. Everybody else has already left for the Bahamas, why do you have to miss all the fun?"

Al shrugged. "Just the luck of the draw."

"Seems like you keep drawing that same unlucky straw" Demetrius saw right through Al's act. Al was the enforcer, so he would always stay behind to do the dirty work.

Angel hopped off the sofa and started wagging her finger in Demetrius' face. "I'm telling you right now, Demetrius Shepherd, if you go to the Bahamas even though you know I can't go, I won't be in this house waiting for you when you get back."

"What you talking about? Where you gon' go?"

"Maybe I'll go back to Frankie. How would you like that?" she countered.

He wouldn't like that at all. Didn't even like the fact that she brought it up. Before he could stop himself, he had grabbed her arm. "Don't you ever throw that name in my face. Don't even say that name in my house. You hear me?"

Her eyes filled with fear as she tried to pry his hand from around her arm. "Let me go, Demetrius."

He caught himself. Their acting had gotten the best of him. He had been about to let jealousy take him somewhere he didn't want to go. And all Angel had done was follow his orders. Demetrius took a deep breath and released her arm. He didn't care that Al was there, he had to make this right. "I'm sorry, Angel. I shouldn't have grabbed your arm. Just don't throw Frankie's name in my face again, okay."

Rubbing her arm, she nodded as she told him, "You didn't have to get so mad. I didn't mean it anyway. You know I'd never go near Frankie."

Al stepped forward. "I hate to break this lover's spat up, but I've got to get this boy to the airport."

"Are we good?" Demetrius ignored Al. He was so afraid that he had just ruined everything and that Angel would never trust him again. He couldn't even go along with their charade until he knew that she was okay.

"I'm cool," she responded. "You just scared me a little bit when you grabbed my arm like that."

"I shouldn't have done it," he admitted.

"And I shouldn't have mentioned Frankie."

"Well then everything is all good in the hood. She'll be here when you get back, Demetrius. So, let's get going," Al told him.

As Demetrius walked out the door, Angel got back into character. "I didn't say I would be here when he got back. Demetrius, I mean it… don't leave."

~~~~~

The moment they left, Angel threw her bags in the back of Demetrius' Bronco. She then put DeMarcus in his car seat and headed to Coach Johnson's house, just as they had planned. Demetrius told her how to get there and Angel only prayed she had remembered the directions correctly. Demetrius wouldn't let her write the directions down for fear that Al would somehow see it and know what was going on.

She pulled up to a ranch style brick house with yellow trimming. "Here goes nothing," she said to DeMarcus as she looked at him through the rearview mirror.

DeMarcus smiled back at her and Angel's heart just melted. No matter how badly things had turned out with Frankie, she would never regret having her son. She took DeMarcus out of his car seat and headed towards the door. Angel remembered Coach Johnson boasting about having a gun, and she prayed that he wouldn't shoot her before she could tell him why she was on his property. Hopefully the baby in her arms would convince him that she came in peace.

She knocked on the door and then waited. She could hear whispering inside the house but no one answered the door. She knocked again as she said, "Can you please open the door, Coach Johnson. Demetrius sent me."

When the door still didn't open, she tried, "Sir, please. It's real important that I speak with you and your wife."

"Look out the window, sir. You'll see that it's just me… well, me and my baby. But we came to help… please let me help you."

Coach Johnson snatched the door open and barked at her. "I remember you from the restaurant. You're in cahoots with them Shepherds, so you need to get from around here before things get ugly."

The gun was in his right hand, he wasn't pointing it at her. Angel spoke slowly, trying to keep the situation calm. "I'm not in cahoots with anyone. I'm here as a favor to Demetrius. He really cares about you and wants to make sure you are okay, sir."

"I just never imagined that Demetrius would stab me and my friends in the back like this," Coach Johnson told her.

Angel took the money Demetrius had given her out of her purse. "This is for you; Demetrius wanted you to have your money back."

"But what about my bet?"

"Please, let me come in so we can talk in private."

Coach Johnson thought about it for a moment and appeared to make a judgement call as he opened the door wide and let her in.

Angel sighed as she put DeMarcus down on the sofa. "There's no easy way to say this, so I'm just going to come out with it. Demetrius thinks you are right. His father did have Professor Green murdered and he thinks the same will happen to you this weekend if you don't get out of here."

"Where am I supposed to go? This is my home."

"Pardon me for saying this sir, but it won't be much of a home if they burn it down."

"That's why I've got this." He lifted his gun. "I'm going to stay up all night, just let 'em try to come in my house."

"I don't think that's a good idea," Angel said. "Demetrius sent me here to pick you and your wife up. He said that you had plans on moving to the South. Well, I'd like to drive you there."

"What?" He gave her an are-you-crazy stare. "Where is Demetrius?"

"He's stalling the man who will be coming after you. I've seen him Coach Johnson. And I can tell you... you don't want this fight. Let me get you out of here."

Coach Johnson paced the floor, thinking... trying to figure the best solution for the problem. Once he stopped pacing he hollered towards the back part of the house. "Katherine, come on out here."

93

Angel smiled at the pretty older woman as she came into the living room. "Hi Mrs. Johnson, my name is Angel."

"Demetrius sent this girl to take you down South. So, go pack your bags and get out of here for a little while."

Her head swiveled on her neck as she turned towards her husband. "Have you lost your complete mind, Sam Winslow Johnson? I am not leaving this house without you."

"You do as I say, Katherine. I had no business gambling away our money." He handed her the stack that Angel had just given him. "At least Demetrius was good enough to get it back for us."

"He gave the money back?" Katherine's eyes filled with tears.

"Demetrius has always been a good boy. I told you that. Now you go with this young girl and let me stay here and take care of the mess I created."

"Where am I supposed to go without you, Sam?" The look on Katherine's face as she asked the question told the whole story. She'd rather die in this house with the man she loved than leave and live without him.

Tears streamed down Angel's face as she watched them. They had the kind of love she always thought her parents had… until they didn't. But this couple had survived the test of time. They were still together after kids and grandkids, and that was the kind of love she wanted. She wasn't going to settle for the fleeting love her parents had, she wanted long, lasting, I'll-stand-here-and-die-with-you kind of love.

Eleven

"I really feel for you, Al. We're all going to be in the Bahamas having the time of our lives and you're stuck here in this boring city."

"Well, don't cry for me. Because when this weekend is over, I'll have so much money that I'll probably lay up in the Bahamas for an entire week."

Demetrius glanced over at Al, and to his horror the man was smiling. He was planning on killing another family this weekend and he was actually smiling. "So, you have no problem with your weekend plans?"

"I'm good. Don't worry about me."

Demetrius pointed to the gas station across the street from the airport terminal. "Pull in there."

"We don't have all day, Demetrius. You don't want to miss your flight."

"I won't miss it. Now pull into the gas station. They got these barbecue skins that I want to snack on while in the air."

"Can't you get some food at the airport?"

"The airport don't sell these skins. So, just pull over. You wanted to be my chauffeur so bad, so get over there and let me get some snacks."

Al shook his head. But he did as Demetrius demanded.

Jumping out of the car, Demetrius glanced at his watch. It was ten-thirty. If Angel had left the house right after him, she should be at Coach's house by now. But, knowing how stubborn Coach was and how angry he had been the last time Demetrius spoke with him, he figured Angel would need a little extra time to persuade him to leave.

So, he did his best imitation of a turtle as he walked down each aisle, picking up a Reese's cup in one aisle, and peanuts in another aisle. Down the chip aisle, Demetrius almost grabbed the bag of Funyuns, but then he remembered that he was supposed to be getting the skins. As he reached for them, Al stormed into the store.

"Grab your stuff and let's go, boy. That plane ain't gone sit on the runway waiting on you."

Demetrius reached down and rubbed his ankle. He looked up at Al and said, "I don't know why, but my ankle is bothering me today. Can you grab some pain pills?"

"Where am I supposed to get that?" Al rolled his eyes in frustration.

"I don't know, go ask the clerk."

~~~

Someone knocked on the door. Sam tried to lift the gun in his hand, but ended up fumbling with it. The gun fell to the ground and as he bent to pick it up, Katherine whispered through tight lips, "You have no business with that gun. You're going to get yourself killed."

The person behind the door said, "Mr. Johnson, it's me, Mark Wilson. There's a big storm coming tonight. I was just checking to see if you wanted me to shovel your snow in the morning."

Breathing a sigh of relief, Sam said, "That'll be fine, Mark. Please shovel the snow in the morning."

As Mark walked away from the house, Angel said, "We don't have much time. Al has probably dropped Demetrius at the airport by now.

Katherine turned back to Sam. "I'm going to pack both of our things and you are leaving this house with me this morning."

"What about the snow that's coming? Someone has to be here to make sure that the house is properly cared for," Sam argued.

But Katherine wasn't hearing any of it. "This house, along with this whole town could freeze over and I wouldn't think twice about it." Wagging a finger at him, she said, "You created this mess, Sam Johnson with that gambling demon you can't seem to shake. I have forgiven you for that. But if you stay here and die... I'll never forgive you and because of the un-forgiveness that will be in my heart when I finally die, I won't see Jesus, and it will all be your fault."

~~~~

They pulled up to the airport at eleven-fifteen, Al was still fussing, "If you miss that flight, I'm going to tell your daddy that it was all because of some barbecue skins."

"Don't worry about it Al. The flight hasn't left yet. But if I miss it, I'll take the heat for it. It's not on you." He patted the man's shoulder trying to reassure him that everything would be alright.

"Okay then." Al calmed down a bit. He got out of the car and helped Demetrius with his bags. "Is your ankle still bothering you? Want me to carry these bags inside?"

97

"Naw, I got it. I guess the pain just comes and goes."

Al, was getting back in the car as he said, "Enjoy yourself. And don't worry about lil' mama. I'll ride past your house and make sure she stays put until you get home."

That was the last thing Demetrius wanted. "She can leave if she wants. After that last comment she made to me, I'm not even sure that I want to deal with her like that anymore."

Al nodded and then grinned, exposing his rotting tooth. "Let me know when you're done with her... I just might like a shot."

Demetrius clamped his mouth shut. The last thing he needed to do was respond to that nonsense. But if Al ever touched Angel, he'd kill the man with his bare hands. He stood there, watching Al pull off. He then went inside the airport and walked over to the Hertz rental car counter.

~~~~

Katherine had managed to convince her husband that they needed to get while the getting was good. But it still took another hour of packing before they had loaded three suitcases and two duffle bags into the Bronco. Sam finally put his foot down as Katherine went back to the house, grabbed a stack of papers and started stuffing them in her purse. "If you don't get out of that house this instant, I'm going to change my mind."

"I'm coming. I'm coming." She dropped a couple of envelopes by the door, she was about to reach down and pick them up, but Sam started hollering.

"Right now, Katherine. We got to get on the road already."

She closed the door, locked it and then got in the SUV.

As Angel drove, Katherine frantically searched through her purse. "I don't have it... it's not here," she said as a single tear dropped from her eyes.

"What's wrong, hon?" Sam asked.

She turned toward him, glaring with accusations. "You rushed me so fast that I left that letter Calvin sent us. It had a picture of our granddaughter in it." This time there was an avalanche of tears.

He held onto his wife trying to soothe away the pain. "Don't be sad. I'll make this right. I promise… If you want, we can come back once everything dies down."

Calming down, she shook her head. "Once we get where we're going, I want you to put this house up for sale. I don't want to live in the same city with Don Shepherd not another day. Calvin will just have to give us another picture of the baby."

"Where do your kids live?" Angel asked as she got onto I-75 South. She was hoping to get them in a conversation that would bring a smile to their faces.

"We were only blessed with one child. A son," Coach Johnson told her. He lives in South Carolina with his wife. They just had a baby girl and Katherine and I planned to spend the summer with them."

Katherine said, "We don't want to burden them. Calvin and his wife are doing really good. The last thing they need is two old fogies to take care of."

"That's why I wanted the money, baby. I knew you wanted to move down South, and if I had a hundred grand I could get you there in style." Coach Johnson lowered his head and sucked in air.

Patting her husband's knee, Katherine tried to console him. "We will still get there, Sam. We've got all of our savings and once we sell the house, we can buy us a small place near Calvin… you and Calvin can go fishing like y'all used to and I can babysit our granddaughter."

"I should have talked to you about this in the first place, now I feel so foolish." His head went low again. "All these years of trying to be an upstanding citizen in our community, and I get us run out of town."

Angel felt for the man. She couldn't let him take all the burden on his shoulders, so she said, "It's not your fault that Demetrius' dad is so greedy that he's willing to kill rather than pay his debts."

"I don't know what's gotten into Don. He's always been a hard man. But he paid up whenever I won the numbers" Shaking his head he added, "If Leo hadn't gotten himself arrested, we wouldn't be in this predicament. Because I would have put my bet in with him."

"I don't like that way of thinking, Sam. You've got to stop all this gambling and I mean it this time. No more, you hear me?"

"After what happened to Danny and his wife, and how sick I've been over it all week. Worried that somebody might come and kill you over a bet I made... you got it, dear. I'm done gambling."

They drove for about fifty miles then pulled into a gas station just before the Cincinnati exit. Angel got out and went to the ladies room. When she came back to the SUV she took a diaper out of her bag and changed DeMarcus.

Coach Johnson kept looking towards that exit; then when Angel got back in and just sat behind the wheel he said, "Don't you think we need to keep moving?"

"Oh, I'm sorry for not communicating what we're doing. Demetrius asked me to meet him at this location. He should be here in a few, I'm sure of it."

"I know you're helping us and all, dear. But I don't think it's wise for us to be left here like sitting ducks," Katherine complained.

"Trust me," Angel began. "If Demetrius says he's going to do something, then it's getting done. He hasn't failed me yet."

"What if he got on the plane and went to the Bahamas instead of risking his neck any further to help us? I've known Demetrius a long time, and he has never defied his father. He's always done what Don told him to, even when it wasn't in his best interest."

"He defied him when he rescued me," Angel said. "I don't want to discuss all the particulars because it's too embarrassing. But his father wasn't happy about Demetrius' choice to help me rather than do exactly what he had been told.

"And," Angel continued, "I don't think you realize how much Demetrius respects and cares for you, Mr. Johnson. He could never stand idly by and let his father hurt you."

"I used to think Demetrius' baseball skills was going to be his ticket out of this town and away from his father. But after he broke his ankle, he just gave up."

"He seems to love the game so much. I would have thought he'd keep trying once his ankle healed. I wonder why he didn't," Angel mused.

"It was all Don's fault. I told him that Demetrius could still get a scholarship to college because his numbers were that good. I said, 'let him heal and then bring him back'. But the man wouldn't hear of it. Told me that Demetrius would never be on that baseball diamond again." Coach just shook his head.

"Maybe Angel came into his life at the right time. And now that he has a son, it's time for Demetrius to realize that he needs to change his life."

Angel gave a half smile as she said, "Maybe… I hope so." She couldn't bring herself to admit that DeMarcus wasn't Demetrius' son. She didn't want this couple, who loved so deeply to know what a fool she had been. And as they kept sitting there waiting on Demetrius, she realized that her mother would want to know about

DeMarcus's father. How could she tell her that she'd left home to shack up with a strip club owner, who dealt drugs to his customers and tried to pimp her out. How could she tell her sweet mother that DeMarcus's father was a heartless man like that?

Just as the shame of the situation was about to overtake her and cause her to rethink this visit with her mother, DeMarcus got fidgety in his seat, as he pointed at something outside and said, "Daddy."

Angel's head swiveled around, 'please God,' she silently prayed. 'Let it be Demetrius'. A silver SUV had just parked next to them. As Angel glanced over with panic in her eyes, she saw that Demetrius was in the driver's seat. Once again he had proven that she could trust him. He hadn't hopped on that plane and left her behind. He got out and then Angel got out and ran to him. She jumped into his arms and sprinkled kisses all over his face.

Laughing, he asked, "What's all of this for?"

"Demetrius Shepherd, you are a man of your word and I love you for that."

Twelve

They took all of the bags out of his SUV and put them in the one he had rented. Angel was confused as to why this had to be done, so she asked, "If I'm going to follow you, why do we need to take our stuff out of your SUV?"

"You and DeMarcus will ride with us. I'm going to leave my SUV here."

"But if you leave it here, somebody might steal it or something," Angel said.

"And if we take it, my father might be able to find us that much faster." He opened the door for her. "Let's go."

Once the women and the baby were in the car, Coach Johnson caught Demetrius by the shoulder and said, "I'm sorry for the way I treated you the other day. I shouldn't have assumed that you knew what your father was up to."

"I'm glad you spoke up," Demetrius told him, and then added, "Look, the real truth is, I don't know if my father is sending someone after you tonight. But if he is, I couldn't live with myself if I just let you die."

"Don isn't going to like this," Coach warned.

That was the understatement of the century, but Demetrius wasn't going to dwell on it. "You told me that you wanted to move south, do you know where you want to go?"

"Columbia, South Carolina," Coach said without giving it a second thought. My son lives there. And with all that's happened, it would do my wife some good to be around the boy and that new grand baby of ours."

"Okay, so we'll drop you there, then I'm taking Angel to Winston-Salem, North Carolina to see her people. I think we'll stay in the South for a week or two. Give my father a little time to cool off."

"What if he pressures you for my location? I don't want anything to happen to my family."

Demetrius put an arm on Coach Johnson's shoulder. "You were good to me when I was a kid. I'll never forget you, Coach… and I'd never tell my father anything about your son. So, don't worry. He won't find you."

They took the back roads out of Ohio into West Virginia. By the time they reached Virginia they were dead tired, so they checked into a hotel. Once Angel, Demetrius and DeMarcus were alone in their room and getting ready for bed, she told him, "I need to talk to you."

Demetrius was carrying DeMarcus on his back. He put him down. "What's up?"

She sat down next to DeMarcus and she said, "I'm kind of embarrassed about this. But Katherine assumed that Mar-Mar is your son, and I didn't correct her."

Demetrius gave her a look that said 'who cares'.

"The thing is, I need a favor from you. And I know that I have no right to ask this, especially since I didn't want you to have anything to do with DeMarcus when we first came to your house."

"Just tell me what you need, Angel. After what you did for me today, I'll move heaven and earth to make you happy."

She smiled at him. He was becoming her hero; she just didn't want to overstep her boundaries and mess up everything. But yet and still, she had to ask. "I told you that I come from a broken home because my father cheated on my mother. But what I didn't tell you is that my father is a preacher."

"He's what? I thought you said the guy was no good?"

"He's not." Angel's mouth tightened as she said, "But that doesn't matter. What does matter, is that despite what my father did, my family is super conservative. It would break my mother's heart to know who DeMarcus's father is."

Lowering her head in shame, she added, "I don't want them to know anything that I've been through, so I'm asking that you pretend that DeMarcus is your son and that we are in love."

He lifted her head with his index finger. When she was looking him in the eye, he said, "We are in love... and DeMarcus already calls me daddy, so I doubt it would be hard to convince them of that."

"So you'll do it?"

He nodded.

Angel wrapped her arms around him. "You are too good to me. Thank you so much."

After the hug, he looked at her for a moment and then said, "Dang girl, why didn't you tell me that your daddy was a preacher. You got me headed to North Carolina not even knowing what I'm about to run into."

"We won't be running into my daddy. I'm not trying to see him. I'm going straight to my mother's little house when we get in town, and that's it."

Al was nervous. He'd just received a 911 call from Don and he didn't want to call him back. The fight had ended badly for Ali. It had been like watching a dead man walking. Al had to close his eyes several times, as he couldn't even stand to watch it from his 13-inch television.

And just as he and Don had planned, once the fight was over, he put a smile on his face, a glock in his right hand and knocked on Coach Johnson's door. In order to get inside, Al was going to tell him that he was there to pay up. Ali had just lost and naturally, Coach would be awaiting his winnings. But no one answered the door.

Al went back to his car and waited and waited, thinking that the Johnson's were out for the evening and would be returning home soon. But then he noticed that Coach's green Buick was parked on the street and hadn't moved from the spot he saw it in yesterday.

Snow had started falling and Al was running low on gas, so he couldn't keep the car running for much longer in order to keep the heat on. He got back out of his car and tried a side window. But all the windows were locked. As he peered into each window however, he didn't notice any movement. Puzzled by this, he knocked on a neighbor's door. Someone peeped out the window but didn't open the door. Al really didn't expect them to open the door. It was dark outside and they lived in the hood. So, he spoke through the window as he pointed toward Coach's house. "I'm trying to find Coach Johnson, but he hasn't been home. Have you seen him?"

The woman responded, "He left," and then closed the curtains.

Al was getting annoyed and when he got annoyed, bad things happened. He took a deep breath and banged on the window. A man came to the window this time, he was angry and brandishing a pistol. He barked, "You want to die tonight?"

Al held up his hands and backed off their porch. "Just looking for Coach Johnson, that's all."

As the snow started falling on Al's head, he realized that he'd just made a bigger mess that he would have to clean up. Because when people realized that the Johnson's were missing, this couple would also remember that he stopped by asking for them. Guess the angry man and his woman would have to die too, Al decided as he crossed the street to his car.

He was just about to get in the car when he noticed a man sitting on his porch fiddling around with a snow blower. "Hey," Al called out to him. "Have you seen Coach Johnson?"

The man looked up, he pointed towards Johnson's house as he said, "They packed up and hightailed it out of here earlier today."

"But his car is still parked over there."

The man glanced at Johnson's car as he said, "They didn't use his car. Some lady picked them up. They drove off in one of them Ford Broncos. And that thing was a beauty, it was black with the oversized tires and rims that sparkled."

He asked the man. "Did that lady have a baby with her?"

The man thought for a second and then bobbed his head. "Sure did."

Al's beeper went off. It was Don again and wasn't no way he could ignore the beep this time. He drove to a phone booth and called the number in his beeper.

When the line was picked up, Don said, "Is that you, Al?"

"It's me." He tried to laugh it off. "Why you keep blowing up my beeper... thought you would be enjoying that tropical island with your new lady."

Don didn't have time for small talk. "Where is Demetrius? Didn't I ask you to get him here?"

"I drove him to the airport myself. But the kid had to stop and buy some barbecue skins for the plane ride."

"What? Demetrius don't eat no skins. He can't stand that stuff."

"Well, that's what he told me. But I swear to you, Don. I dropped him off at the airport in enough time to make his flight."

"What about the girl?"

"She decided to stay here because they couldn't find a babysitter."

Don sucked in his teeth. But then quickly got down to another matter. "Ali lost, can you believe it… I just hope I haven't lost too much money because I've already lined up our next project, but we're going to need a ton of loot to get in on it."

Al knew that Don was looking for reassurance that Coach had been taken care of, and he could see his bonus slipping through his fingers as he said, "We got a problem over here."

"Yeah, what sort of problem?" Don asked.

"You see, I went to visit a sick friend. But when I arrived at his house, he was gone."

"Gone… what do you mean, gone? Don't you know your friend's schedule?"

"That's just it," Al said, "I've been over this way for a week straight. Everything stayed the same. Only today is different… and the neighbor told me…"

"You talked to the neighbor? What are you a freakin' idiot? I mean really, did your mommy dress you this morning?" Don exploded.

"I know I shouldn't be talking to these people, Don. But I've got extenuating circumstances going on."

"Like what?"

"Like… somebody drove Sam and his wife out of here in a black Ford Bronco."

"Demetrius drives a Bronco," Don said.

"Exactly." Al had gotten played. He could accept that. But now, Don was going to have to do something about his kid once and for all.

"You think Demetrius has something to do with this?"

"You said he didn't make it to the Bahamas, and I took him to the airport myself. And now this man describes Demetrius' Bronco down to the rims. He also told me that a woman with a kid picked the Johnson's up."

"I'll kill him," Don exploded again. "Drive over to his house and see if he's got them over there."

Al did as he was told. The first thing he noticed when he pulled up to Demetrius' house was that the Bronco was gone. He got out of his car and knocked on the door. But of course, there was no answer. Al ran back over the scene in the house when he'd picked Demetrius up that morning. The two of them were angry one moment, consoling one another the next and then like a faucet they switched back to being angry.

If it hadn't been Don Shepherd's kid, Al would have recognized the set up and acted right then and there. He called Don back and told him what he'd found.

There was silence on the phone, then Don said, "So my son has gone rogue, huh?"

"It appears that way. Demetrius spent a lot of time with Coach Johnson when he was growing up. Maybe he feels he owes Coach his loyalty."

"Demetrius is my son," Don barked. "His loyalty belongs to me… to the family."

"What do you want me to do?" Al asked waiting on his orders.

"I want you to find them. I'm going to show Demetrius who his daddy really is, and then I guarantee that boy will never choose anyone over his family again."

Thirteen

Al and his crew went through the Johnson's home looking for anything that might give a clue as to where they had ran off to. The bedrooms were ransacked, as if they had packed in a hurry and decided to leave what they didn't want on the floor.

"Hey Al, come check this out," one of his henchmen said.

Al was in the kitchen making himself a turkey sandwich. He put the mustard back in the refrigerator and headed to the living room while eating his sandwich.

The man handed him an envelope and said, "This was laying by the front door. I think they dropped it on their way out."

Al opened the envelope and found the picture of a cute little baby girl, and a letter that had been sent from their son. He looked at the front of the envelope and then smiled… he had an address. He called Don because he had two things to report.

When Don picked up the phone, the first thing Al said was, "The Bronco is parked at a gas station just outside of Cincinnati."

"How long has it been there?"

"A few hours."

Don let out one explicative after another. Then he said, "I should set that truck on fire to teach him a lesson."

"Say the word and I'll have it torched tonight. But I've got something else. We just found an address for Coach Johnson's son."

"Where does he live?" Don asked.

"Columbia, South Carolina."

"Alright then, have a couple of our guys pay him a visit."

"Don't you want me to go check on this myself?" Al asked.

But Don said, "No, not yet. I want you to sit tight. I'm flying back tonight. My son isn't going to spit in my face like this and just ride off into the sunset. So, I expect you to have some answers when I get there. Understand?"

"Yeah boss, I got it." Al hung up the phone without saying anything else, but he was boiling on the inside. The boss's kid goes rouge and suddenly it's his fault. Don is the one who brought him into the business... should have let that boy go to college or something. Because he didn't look forward to hunting down the son of Don Shepherd.

~~~~

As Saul touched down on earth, he closed his wings and adapted to his human form. Today he was working as a carrier for a local travel company. Saul had a very special package to deliver to the Executive Vice President of a small but growing tech firm. Garland Hansbro ran the marketing department and Calvin Johnson reported directly to him as Director of Marketing.

"I have a package for Mr. Hansbro," Saul informed the receptionist.

Without looking up from her desk, she held out her hand. "Give it to me. I'll make sure he gets it."

Shaking his head, Saul said, "I was told that only Mr. Hansbro could sign for this package."

The woman turned her head towards Saul, she looked, up, up and up. "My, aren't we tall. What happened, did you blow your knee out or something?"

"Huh?" Saul didn't understand the woman.

"You should be on somebody's basketball court, dunking on poor defenseless seven footers. What are you doing delivering packages?"

Smiling, Saul said, "It's my job ma'am."

She pointed to a group of chairs that lined the wall. "Have a seat, I'll see if Mr. Hansbro is available."

Within five minutes, the receptionist informed him that Mr. Hansbro would see him. She led him through a cubicle filled room. They turned a corner and Saul was greeted by a long line of offices. Mr. Hansbro's office was at the far end. The man's office was spacious with ceiling to floor windows that provided a perfect city view.

Hansbro was 6'7. He stood up and shook Saul's hand. "I need you to stick around for a little while so my team can stop thinking that I'm some freak of nature."

"I get that all the time," Saul told him. But inside he was reminding himself to work on the height issue next time he needed to be seen on earth.

Saul handed over the package. "I just need you to sign for this."

"What is it?" Hansbro asked, as he took the package.

"It's an all-expense paid trip to Myrtle Beach this weekend, for you and your wife. My company would like to meet with executives to show off our newly renovated resort. It's the perfect place for an employee retreat because we not only have golf, dining and swimming; but we have several meeting rooms for break-out sessions or large employee meetings."

"Sounds great, I'd love to go." Hansbro was getting excited. But then the light in his eyes slowly flickered out. "But my wife and I have plans with the kids this weekend. I wish this wasn't so last minute."

"You can bring the kids along. Why don't you give your wife a call and see if she can rearrange some things."

Hansbro was back to beaming. "If we can bring the kids, I'm sure she will want to go."

"And if she doesn't," the receptionist spoke up, "I'd be more than happy to take that package off your hands." She tried to laugh it off, but she was serious.

Hansbro got his wife on the phone, but she wasn't having it. Saul could hear her scream through the phone, something about, "you always break your word to these kids. As far as I'm concerned, Gary's baseball game and Brianna's recital are more important than some fake vacation that will just turn out to be about business and not about the family at all."

"What am I supposed to do with this package? It's totally free and you're just going to pass that up?" Hansbro pleaded.

"Yes, let's pass it up. Give it to one of your executives and let them check the place out. If it turns out to be as wonderful as this guy says, then you and I can go there after Gary's last game this season."

Saul smiled as Hansbro hung up the phone. Hansbro looked confused by the fact that his wife would pass this trip up. But Hansbro didn't know about the angel Saul had dispatched to his home earlier that morning who'd convinced her that children come first, vacations can wait.

Shaking his head, Hansbro said, "It's a no go. But thanks so much for thinking of us."

"You really don't want to pass this up, Mr. Hansbro," Saul said. "Do you have another person you would feel comfortable sending on the trip?"

The receptionist was jumping up and down, with her hand raised. "Pick me… pick me."

"I'm sorry," he told her. "If it's an executive trip, I have to send one of my directors."

She stopped jumping and put her hand down. "I understand."

"Can you ask Calvin Johnson to come to my office, please," Hansbro told her.

Saul looked to heaven. He could feel Captain Aaron's eyes on him as the mission was about to be completed. Katherine Johnson was a praying woman, she'd covered her son in prayer since he was a child. So, Saul wasn't going to let Don Shepherd get his hands on what belonged to God.

~~~~

Demetrius and the gang went to Denny's for breakfast as soon as they woke the next morning. They were laughing and joking with each other as if they were on vacation, rather than running for their lives. But laughter was good like a medicine, so they laughed on.

Coach and Katherine excused themselves from the table. They wanted to find a pay phone so they could call their son to let him know they were coming for a visit.

Once they were gone, Angel asked Demetrius, "What do you think is happening back home?"

He leaned back in his seat, thought about it for a moment. "My father has figured out that I didn't get on the plane. They're probably looking for me… I wouldn't doubt if they've found my SUV by now."

"But how, we didn't leave it in Dayton."

"My father has connections all over Ohio. He'll find it." Demetrius' lip twisted as he added, "I should have left the key in it. Lord knows what they'll do to my SUV if they can't drive it."

"What do you think your dad will do about Coach Johnson?"

"Once they see that Coach Johnson doesn't plan to come back to town, Dad will let it go. There's no reason to kill Coach if he's not asking for his money, right?"

"Right," Angel agreed as she put her hand over Demetrius' hand. "I don't think I even thanked you for what you're doing."

"You don't need to thank me, Coach means a lot to me."

She shook her head. "I'm not just talking about what you're doing for Mr. and Mrs. Johnson. I want to thank you for keeping your word about taking me home to see my mother."

"Girl, when are you going to realize that I am a man of my word?"

"I'm starting to get it. But forgive me for being a little slow to catch on. I haven't had many examples of men who keep their word." Her eyes filled with sadness as she added. "I used to be able to count on my father, but then he changed."

Coach Johnson and Katherine slid back into the booth.

Demetrius asked them, "Did you talk to your son?"

Katherine shook her head. "No one answered. I even called his office because he works at least one Saturday out of the month, but no one answered the phone there either."

"Maybe he's just out for breakfast like us," Angel said. "I'm sure they will be home by the time we get there."

~~~~

Angel nodded off in the car. As she slept she kept hearing someone tell her, "Don't go to Colombia, you need to go home first." Over and over she heard those words until she was jolted out

116

of her sleep. She saw the sign for Winston-Salem and pointed at it, "Turn off here."

Demetrius's brow rose. "We're going to Columbia first, remember?"

Vigorously shaking her head, Angel told him. "I've got a real bad feeling about this. We need to go to Winston-Salem before we drop the Johnson's off. I don't know why, but I feel it in my gut."

"That might be God trying to tell you something," Katherine said. "I know a lady who gets premonitions. I think we should take the next exit," Katherine said firmly.

Demetrius took the exit to get off the highway.

Angel had Demetrius drive over by the Wake Forest University Resident Hall. Since her mother divorced her father, all she'd been able to afford was rent on a seven hundred square foot, two bedroom home that the college students didn't even want.

"Your mom lives here?" Demetrius asked.

Angel nodded. "When dad left, he took his money with him." The sadness in her voice must have been thick, because Katherine reached from the back and put a hand on her shoulder.

"Don't you worry about that. God has a way of taking care of the injustices of this world. I've trusted Him all my life, and won't stop until they put me six feet under."

Angel was astonished by Katherine's statement. The woman was fleeing for her life because her husband was a gambler, but she still trusted in God. Meanwhile, Angel had lost her faith and trust years ago.

Angel was nervous about seeing her mother after being gone for so many years, but somehow Katherine's presence gave her the strength she needed to see this through. "Thank you for allowing us to come to Winston-Salem before driving on to Columbia. I know you want to see your own family, but it means a lot to me to have you are here."

Katherine smiled at Angel and she said, "I'm enjoying my road trip with you, so don't give it a second thought. Now you go see your mother. She's waited a long time for this moment. Don't make her wait any longer."

Angel got out of the SUV and slowly walked up to the house. She hesitated a moment as all of her brokenness replayed itself in her head. She was still so very ashamed of what she had become. But this was her mother, she wouldn't judge her… just love her, because that's what moms do. She shook the nervousness off and knocked on the door.

A tall black boy wearing a Wake Forest University jersey opened the door and stared at her.

"Um… I'm looking for Maxine Barnes."

He kept staring, but said nothing.

"She's my mother," Angel explained further. "She lives here with my brother Ronny."

"I don't know what you're talking about. There's no Maxine or Ronny here. This is my house. I'm a medical student at Wake Forest."

Deflated, Angel got back in the SUV and told them. "She doesn't live here anymore. My own mother moves and I didn't know anything about it."

"When's the last time you spoke with your mother?" Coach Johnson asked.

"I left home when I was sixteen. So, it's been almost three years. But I always pictured her here in this house, peering out the window, waiting on the day I decided to come back home. But I guess they moved on without me."

The door to the house opened and the guy she'd spoken to ran over to the car. He knocked on the driver's side window and Demetrius rolled it down.

"One of my buddies knows your mom," he told Angel. "He said she's normally at Full Gospel Church on Saturdays and Sundays."

"But that's my father's church," Angel said, thinking that there was some kind of mistake.

~~~~

"Ain't nobody home, Al. The beds are made, no dishes in the sink. I don't think they've been home all night. But nothing in the house indicates they had travel plans. Because most people leave something in the trash, on the table or a desk with hotel or flight info. We didn't find a thing."

Al was holding the phone listening to the report. He bit into the tooth pick he had been picking his teeth with and spat it on the ground. "Okay, just stake out the place for a while to see if his son shows up."

Don was standing next to Al as he hung up the phone. "Nothing?"

"Like they just disappeared or something," Al confirmed.

"Maybe Sam called and told his kid to get out of dodge." Don's lip curled in anger as he crumpled up the cup of coffee he'd been drinking and threw it in the trash. "You know what burns me up? When Demetrius was a kid, Johnson was always patting him on the back… giving him "atta boys" for practically nothing. So, now my kid thinks that Johnson is some great guy, and I'm just the scum who put clothes on his back and made sure he didn't go hungry."

"Always some Do-gooder getting in the middle of family business and messing things up."

"Exactly," Don agreed. "But this time Johnson is going to pay for causing my boy to disrespect me like this."

Al was down for whatever. He said, "What do you think we should do next?"

"Let's go visit Mo. See if Demetrius confided in his friend."

Fourteen

Angel had been twelve years old the last time she stepped foot inside Full Gospel Church. It was the day that her parents announced to the church that they were divorcing. Her brother had only been ten at the time, but even so, he and Angel held onto each other and bawled their eyes out. When they wouldn't stop crying, her dad, the great pastor of Full Gospel Church had asked the ushers to remove them from their spot on the front pew.

He'd acted as if they had done something wrong, when all the time it had been him. He had been the one who cheated. He had been the one who hadn't even fought for his marriage, just allowed her mom to throw him out. She had vowed that day, as she and her brother had been relegated to a back room so that the congregation wouldn't see just how badly his actions had torn up the family, that she would never step foot into this church again.

But what Angel didn't understand is why her mother had come back? The guy at their old house said that her mother was here every Saturday and Sunday. Why? Angel didn't have long to ponder the question, because when she opened the doors to the sanctuary she saw her mother behind the pulpit. She wasn't standing though, she was seated in a chair, her voice booming as she talked passionately to a crowd of about a hundred people;

Maxine Barnes was saying, "I thank each and every one of you as we all stand together against the sex trade that is going on, not only in faraway countries, but also in our own land. We might have children who are out there lost and being forced to sell their bodies, but I truly believe that God is smiling down on us as we work to rescue other children out of this land of darkness. And one day, we too shall be reunited with our own children.

"So, as we head out again today, please remember, that what you do for someone else, God will make happen for you. Ever since the day my niece told me that my little girl was trapped in a world of prostitution, I've been on the battle field. It's been many years, but I still believe that God will answer my prayers. Do you believe it too?" she shouted out the question.

Those in attendance raised their hands and shouted back, "I believe."

Katherine whispered in Angel's ear. "I don't think she forgot about you."

"But she's got it all wrong," Angel protested. "I'm not a prostitute."

"You don't know what the devil would have gotten you into on them streets if it hadn't been for your mother praying." Katherine told her.

Oh yes, Angel was well aware of the many things 'the devil' had gotten her involved in and the things Demetrius had saved her from. But now she wondered if Demetrius had been the one to save her or if it had been her mother's prayers. She immediately scratched that thought, because if God had wanted to do something for her, He could have done it when she was twelve years old and constantly praying that her parents would get back together.

"Grab a stack of pamphlets as you head out today. Those girls might be afraid to talk to us for fear that their pimp might see them. But if they read the pamphlet, it tells them where to go for shelter."

Angel then noticed that her mother was slow to stand. She pointed at something towards the front pew and then her father ran up to the podium with a cane. Maxine then used the cane to stand up and then her father helped her down the three steps.

"What happened to my mother?"

Demetrius thought Angel was asking the question of him, he shook his head as he asked, "She wasn't using a cane before you left?"

"Not at all. She was very active and vibrant." Angel didn't wait any longer, she handed DeMarcus to Demetrius and then rushed down the aisle to see about her mother.

Maxine's head lifted as she descended the last step. Her voice could be heard through the sanctuary as she screamed, "Oh my Lord. It's my baby. She's come home… Thank You, Jesus. Angel has come back home!"

~~~~

Demetrius gave them a minute, then he and DeMarcus followed Angel down the aisle. As he got closer he heard Angel say to her mom, "I'm not a prostitute, why are you telling people that I am?"

Her mother looked confused. Her arm had been around Angel. It dropped as she looked into Angel's eyes, as if she would find the truth within the depths of those beautiful brown eyes. "The week your cousin went to jail, she called her mother asking for money. I drove my sister all the way to Dayton so we could visit her. I begged her to tell me where you were. But she said she didn't know… told me that some man was taking you from city to city selling you for money."

Demetrius shook his head. When you can't trust family, you can't trust nobody. Angel could have already been home with her mother, if that snake in the grass had just been honest. He reached the group and handed DeMarcus to Angel. She smiled at him.

Angel switched DeMarcus from one hip to the other. She then turned to her mom. "I came home because I wanted to introduce you to your grandson."

Maxine and Marvin were both silent as they stared at the toddler. But then Maxine reached out. "Can I hold him?"

Angel handed DeMarcus over to her mother as she told him, "Go to your grandmother."

Maxine light heartedly corrected her. "He can call me Nana. I'm too young to be called grandmother."

Meanwhile, Marvin was looking directly at Demetrius. His beeper had gone off twice while he was standing with them. He'd glanced at it and saw that Mo was sending him 911 signals. He ignored it and hooked the beeper back to his pants.

Then Marvin asked his daughter, "Who is this young man standing next to you, Angel?"

Angel's eyes shone with love as she looked up at Demetrius. She put an arm around his waist as she gulped hard and then said, "This is my fiancé. I know that we've done things a little backward by having DeMarcus first. But don't worry, because we will be getting married very soon." Her face looked like it would break from smiling so hard as she told those lies.

Demetrius' beeper went off again. He wanted to ignore this one also, but Mo put the 333 code in this time. That was their signal for distress. Mo was in trouble, so Demetrius had to reach out to him.

"Just what do you do, young man?" Marvin asked with a look on his face that said he knew the deal.

But Demetrius didn't have time to get into it with Angel's father. Mo needed him and he had to get to a phone ASAP. "I'm sorry, Pastor Barnes, I will tell you whatever you want to know about me, but right now I really need to make a call. Can I possibly use your phone?"

Pastor Barnes pointed in the direction of his office. "My office is on the other side of those double doors. Help yourself."

"Thank you," Demetrius said as he attempted to walk past the group. But DeMarcus reached for him.

"Daddy," he said as he held out his hands.

He looked to Angel and she said, "Go on, take him with you." Then she turned back to her parents. "That boy just can't stand being without his daddy."

If he hadn't had other things weighing on his mind, Demetrius would have laughed his head off once he'd closed the office door. Angel hadn't even wanted him anywhere near DeMarcus when they had first come to stay with him... now she's lying her head off, telling anyone who will listen that he was DeMarcus's dad.

He sat the boy on the floor as he dialed Mo's number, Demetrius figured he already knew what the problem was, he just hoped that Mo was alright.

DeMarcus was playing with the long spiral phone cord as Mo answered the phone.

Demetrius said, "What's up, man? You in some kind of trouble?"

"Your daddy is losing it, Demetrius. They pretty near beat me to death up in here. And Don said they're going to kill me if you don't put in a call to him in the next hour."

Mo sounded scared, God only knows what they had done to him. "Put him on the phone."

"He's not here. I think him and Al are headed to Frankie Day's house. They're trying to find out where Angel's people stay."

"But if I put this number in his beeper, he'll know where Angel's people are."

"And if you don't, my people won't know where to find me. Because I'll be floating in a river somewhere."

Don wasn't giving him much of a choice. He had to call, but nothing said that he had to call from Winston-Salem. Demetrius stepped out of the office and signaled for Angel to come to him. When she was in front of him, he handed her DeMarcus and then said, "I have to leave."

"But my father wants to talk to you."

Stepping closer to her, so that only she heard him, Demetrius said, "I don't have a choice. My father is going to kill Mo if I don't call him within the next hour. So, I've got to get on the road now. Because I don't want to call him from Winston-Salem."

"Gotcha. Okay, you go." she was whispering with him. "I'll make sure Katherine and Sam get something to eat."

"Where are they?" Demetrius asked, he hadn't seen them since Angel had gone down the aisle to see her mother.

"They're sitting on one of the back pews. I saw them when I handed DeMarcus to mama."

He kissed her and then left the building. He made it as far as Concord before pulling off the highway at breakneck speed. He pulled into the first gas station he came to, and called his father's beeper. He then stood at the phone booth and waited for the phone to ring. After ten minutes had gone by, Demetrius began to worry that he'd called too late and that Mo was already dead. Just as he was about to pick the phone receiver up and call Mo's number the phone rang.

He quickly picked it up. "Hello… hello."

"I'm here. I just need a minute because I'm still in shock that a son of mine would defy me in such a manner."

"Dad, is Mo okay?"

"He's still breathing if that's what you mean."

Demetrius sighed in relief. "Let me speak to him."

Don laughed. "Don't trust your old man, huh? Well, you can call him yourself when we hang up. But I think he went to the emergency room about a broken rib or something."

"Mo had nothing to do with it, Dad. You shouldn't have hurt him."

Don's voice was like steel as he said, "I want Johnson back here. I owe him money so, I need to settle up."

"You don't owe him anything, Dad. I gave him his money back. He's not looking for a pay out on that bet. They just want to sell their home so they can relocate."

Don pondered that a moment, then he asked, "And you believe that? Johnson is going to call the police and tell them everything he knows the moment you drop him at his son's house in Columbia. You know that don't you?"

"You know where his son lives?" Demetrius didn't even know why he was surprised.

"Already sent someone to the house, but no one was home. Now why don't you ask Johnson how long he thinks my people should wait on his son to return?"

"What's that supposed to mean?" Demetrius was horrified by his father's statement, but he tried to keep his voice calm.

"You know me, Demetrius. What do you think I mean? Better yet, what do you think I'm going to do next?"

"But he doesn't want the money." It seemed like his dad didn't even care about the money anymore, like he was mad about something else. But Demetrius didn't understand it at all.

"Oh and tell Pastor Barnes that I said hello. I might even attend services real soon."

Nooo! Demetrius wanted to scream. His father had found them in no time at all. There was nowhere to run, nowhere to hide from Don Shepherd. "Why can't you just leave us alone? Coach doesn't want the money, so that should be the end of it."

"He took something that belongs to me and somebody's got to pay for that."

"This isn't about you, Dad. I just didn't want Coach to die over a bet that he never should have made in the first place. Don't you get that?"

"You seem to have forgotten where your money comes from… and you go against me for some chump." Pure anger spilled from Don's voice as he continued. "Maybe I should do to you exactly what I'm going to do to Johnson's kid when I get my hands on him." Don hung up the phone.

Demetrius got back in his car and slumped against the steering wheel. He'd thought that once his father understood that Coach didn't want the money, he would leave him alone, but Don wasn't going to stop. Demetrius had driven an hour out of the way, just so his father wouldn't know where they were. But Frankie must have known about Angel's father and happily spilled the beans.

If Don wasn't going to stop hunting them, then Demetrius had no clue how he was going to keep them safe. But one thing was clear to him, he had to get back to Winston-Salem immediately.

Fifteen

By the time Demetrius arrived back in Winston-Salem, everyone had left the church. Angel had beeped him, he called her back and she gave him directions to her parent's home. She ran outside and got in the passenger seat as he pulled into the driveway.

"So, did we set a date for the wedding while I was gone," Demetrius said, needing desperately to laugh about something.

"Thanks for not busting me out in front of my parents."

"I should have," he told her. "You had me co-signing all them lies right in the sanctuary of your father's church. Woman, do you have no fear of God?"

Leaning back in her seat, Angel admitted, "What I did wasn't right. But a whole lot of things haven't been right for a long time."

"Yeah," he agreed. "What your cousin did was foul."

"That wasn't even the worst of it, Demetrius. After you left, I asked my mom why she was walking with a cane." Shaking her head in disbelief, Angel said, "My mom had a stroke after my cousin lied to her like that."

"That's why she and my father got back together. He felt so guilty for all he had done, that he stepped down as pastor of the church for about six months and took care of her. My mom said she fell back in love with my dad during that time. And they remarried last year."

"Yeah, well at least some good came out of it."

Angel looked doubtful. "That's if he can stop letting these church hussies fill his head with how wonderful he is and stay faithful to his wife."

"And you don't believe he can?"

"My mother seems to believe it. And I guess that's all that matters. She's been through so much already, I don't want to rain on her party. So, I'm going to try my best to keep my mouth shut."

"Good, because we have bigger issues." He turned to her, held onto her hands as he said, "I think Frankie told my father about your family. He knows that he is a preacher and he told me that he's planning a visit to the church. So, he thinks that we're with your family."

"We are with my family, Demetrius." Angel's hands tightened around his. "What are we going to do?"

"I don't know. Let's just go inside. I need to talk to Coach and then I'll figure something out."

"My father wants to talk to you too," Angel said, then grabbed hold of his arm. "But you can't tell my father about any of this."

"Why not... are you ashamed of your fiancé?" he teased her, but in truth, Demetrius needed an answer to that. He was who he was, and if the woman he loved couldn't deal with that, then...

"I'm not ashamed of you, Demetrius. You're a good man. And I'm proud to be on your arm. Now come on in the house so we can figure out what to do."

Demetrius was intrigued the moment he stepped onto the veranda and then walked through the front doors. The house was a Victorian style that southerners seemed to love. At the front of the house the parlor and drawing room was used to showcase pictures. These pictures were unlike any he'd ever seen in anyone else's home. On one of the walls was five photos of men dressed in dark suits, holding a bible. Each man had a clerical collar around his neck.

Of the five, the last picture was of Angel's father. So, Demetrius asked, "Who are the rest of these men?"

She pointed at the pictures. "The picture next to my father is of my grandfather, then my great grandfather... great, great, grandfather and so on."

He whispered, "Does everybody in your family preach?"

"Pretty much," Angel said as she led him towards the back of the house where the family room and kitchen were. Katherine was in the kitchen helping Maxine with the dinner. Coach was seated in the family room with Angel's dad watching television and kicking back with a tall glass of lemonade.

Before Demetrius could take a seat on the antique, Victorian style sofa, Coach asked him, "Did you get everything squared away?"

"Not quite," Demetrius admitted. "You might want to call your son to see if he's made it back home yet."

Coach jumped up. "Don't tell me that Don knows where Calvin lives?" His eyes begged Demetrius to say it wasn't so.

But Demetrius couldn't lie to him. "They sent someone to his house already. So, Angel was right when she told us not to make your son's house our first stop."

Katherine wiped her hands with the kitchen towel as she came into the room. "Has that monster hurt my son?" She looked from her husband to Demetrius, needing an answer quick and fast.

Demetrius shook his head. "No ma'am. No one is at Calvin's home. But you need to find out where he is and advise him to stay there for a few more days."

Johnson asked Marvin, "Can I use your phone?"

Marvin told him, "There's a phone in the kitchen and one in the parlor." As Coach and Katherine headed to the kitchen, Marvin set his eyes on Demetrius. "I think it's time for us to talk, don't you?"

"I think so," Demetrius agreed as he sat down across from Pastor Marvin. Angel sat next to him, and he appreciated that. His father had been so worried that he had fallen for a girl who wouldn't be down for him. But Angel was the one. He was glad she had told her parents that they were engaged, because he wanted to spend the rest of his life with this girl.

"Before I begin, I want you to know that I love your daughter, and although I'm not the best possible candidate for a son-in-law, I don't think anyone will treat her better than I will."

"That's all well and good, young man. But exactly how do you plan to provide for Angel and DeMarcus? What do you do for a living?"

"I work for my father, sir. And I could try to pretty that up, but I'm not going to lie to you." Demetrius took a deep breath as he continued. "My father's business is organized crime. We make our living as bookies and loan sharks." The business was about to transform into drug dealing, but he didn't feel like sharing that bit of information just yet.

"And you think that you're worthy of Angel, even though you're nothing more than a criminal?"

Angel held onto his hand and squeezed it, reassuring him that she was still with him.

"No, sir. I'm far from worthy. But I still want to be with her." He looked into Angel's eyes as he said, "We want to be a family."

"But you can't raise a family if you are in prison," Marvin exploded. "This is non-sense."

Angel glared at her father and then went on the attack. "You have no room to judge Demetrius. Not when you ran off with some other woman while mama was left to take care of me and Ronny in some shack on the other side of town." She stood up, shaking a finger in her father's face. "You can't raise a family like that either, can you?"

"Angel!" The displeasure in her mother's voice rang throughout the room. "You have no right to speak to your father like that."

Angel took a couple of deep slow breaths. She sat back down next to Demetrius as she told her mother, "I'm sorry. I will not disrespect your home again. But your husband has no right talking to Demetrius like that."

"He's only concerned for your well-being," Maxine told her.

Before Angel could say another word, Johnson rushed back into the room. "I got in touch with his boss. Calvin's safe. He took the family to the beach for the weekend."

"Safe from what?" Marvin asked. "Does anyone want to tell me what's going on?"

~~~~

Stan, Al, Joe-Joe and Don flew into Smith Reynolds Airport and rented two cars. Don kept Al with him, because he didn't want his enforcer getting any ideas about shooting his son, unless he gave the order for such a thing. Joe-Joe and Stan got into the other car. It was late Saturday evening, the sun was going down as they headed out to find the church and/or the pastor's home if need be.

Winston-Salem was a small little college town, with Wake Forest University and Winston-Salem State University, along with several other smaller colleges. It was a place for higher learning, which was why Don was surprised to see young thugs hanging out on the street when there was practically a college on every other block. They pulled up to the Full Gospel Church and got out of the car. Don and Al leaned against the car and waited on Stan and Joe-Joe to pull up next to them.

"What's this," Joe-Joe said as he closed his car door. "We leave our ghetto to come hang out in theirs?"

"We should have found the house, I bet you that preacher don't live in this neighborhood. And the church looks like it's closed for the day anyway," Al said.

"We couldn't get an address on the preacher," Don reminded him. "But we'll find him."

~~~~

"So you're telling me that you're father wants to kill a man so he won't have to pay money owed for a bet? And you and my daughter have risked your lives to save this man?" Pastor Marvin couldn't believe what he was hearing.

"When my father gets angry, there's no telling what he will do."

"And yet you decided to defy him in order to help the Johnson's anyway," Maxine said as if she was beginning to see what her daughter saw in him.

"Coach Johnson means a lot to me. When I was a kid, he was more of a father figure to me than my father ever thought about being."

"I appreciate your saying that, Demetrius." Sam put a hand on his back. "I tried to be there for you because I could see that you were hurting without your mother." Johnson then turned to Pastor Marvin and said, "Don Shepherd has to be stopped before he destroys anymore lives."

Pastor Marvin clasped his hands as he stood up. "I know someone who can stop him."

Demetrius shook his head. "If I call the police on my father he would never forgive me. I'd probably be found dead somewhere."

"I'm not talking about any earthly authority," Pastor Marvin told them. Then as their eyes got that puzzled look, he pointed upward. "I'm talking about Jesus. My Lord and Savior is the only one I trust with my life."

Angel remembered her father saying things like this when she was a child. He had always inspired her to trust God for anything. But then he messed up and it had changed her whole outlook on faith and God's ability to rescue her from anything.

Pastor Marvin got down on his knees, Maxine joined him and so did Katherine and Johnson. Demetrius whispered to Angel, "What should I do?"

She put his hand in hers and then got down on bended knee, getting the picture, Demetrius followed suit.

Pastor Marvin began praying, "Father God, we give thanks to You and You alone for Your mighty hand that is quick to save and to deliver. Only You know the true depths of the danger my daughter and her friends are facing this weekend. So I come to You now, asking that You put a hedge of protection around them that no evil force will be able to penetrate.

"And if these evil men cannot be persuaded to stop their pursuit of this good man and his family, then Lord I ask that You stop them in such a way that they will never look to this part of the country ever again. Send down warrior angels to fight this battle for us, in Jesus's name I pray."

As Pastor Marvin ended his prayer, Maxine began, "And Lord, my Lord, I just want to thank You for bringing my daughter back to us safe and sound just as You promised during the many nights of seeking You through my tears. I thank You that not one tear was shed in vain and I thank You for the additions to our family. Watch over DeMarcus and Demetrius, Lord. As DeMarcus grows, send someone to teach him about You, so that he may one day serve You in spirit and in truth. And Father, I pray that Demetrius and Angel come to know You as their Lord and savior, and that they come to know what it truly means to walk up right before You. Whatever You have to do, Lord, do it to bring them in line."

Demetrius wanted to stop the praying session. First, Pastor Marvin prayed for God to do something to his daddy and then his wife was praying for God to do something to him. He didn't like any of it. He tried to stand up, but he felt like some force in the room was holding him down. Then he felt pressure on the back of his neck as his head bent against his will also.

Maxine then concluded her prayer with, "In Jesus's holy and un-matchless name I pray."

The weight lifted off of Demetrius and he was able to lift his head and stand up. He looked around to see if anyone was behind him, but no one was there. Something weird had just happened to him, and somebody needed to explain it, so he asked Pastor Marvin, "Who was holding me down?"

"Excuse me?" Pastor Marvin looked just as confused as Demetrius.

"I tried to get up while y'all were praying, but some kind of force kept me on my knees, and then somebody put pressure on my neck to make me bow my head."

Grinning as if he knew a secret and wasn't about to tell it, Marvin steepled his hands and looked to heaven. "Thank You, Father, for I know that You always hear us, when we pray." Then he squeezed his wife's hands and as they lovingly looked into each other's eyes, he added, "For where two or three are gathered together in His name, He is there in the midst of them."

"Amen for that," Maxine said.

But Demetrius was standing there looking at them as if they had flown over a coo-coo's nest. "What are they talking about?"

Angel hadn't read her Bible in a long time, but she hadn't forgotten that scripture. "It's a scripture out of the book of Matthews," she told him.

"The book of who?"

Angel let out a long suffering sigh as she turned to Demetrius. "You have a Bible in the top drawer of your dresser. Are you telling me that you've never read it?"

When he didn't respond, with agitation in her voice, Angel said, "Just forget it. The book of Matthews is in the Bible, and my parents are trying to say that they believe God was here with us as they prayed."

"Well, why didn't they just say that? These people are weird." Demetrius shrugged his shoulders, still looking behind him, trying to make sure that nothing else was about to happen to him in this house.

Angel went upstairs to check on DeMarcus.

~~~~

If Saul had a feather he would have brushed it across Demetrius' nose just to spook him a bit more. The boy needed the fear of God, because the way his life was going, Saul just didn't see how he and Angel could raise up a child that was going to usher in the last day revival. But that wasn't his business. He was there to watch over Demetrius and Angel, and he would do just that.

And even without calling the Arc Angel, Michael's name, by praying for warrior angels, Pastor Marvin had released heaven to fight this battle. Saul felt a comfort in that, because he would not have to deal with the enemy alone. Even now, he could hear the sound of warriors marching this way.

Sixteen

They had been driving around the city for over an hour, getting lost at every turn. Finally, they made it back on the side of town where Full Gospel Church was. Don said, "Pull over."

"Why, what's up? You see something?" Al asked as he put on his signal to get over.

"Yeah, pull into that gas station."

Al pulled into the station and then spoke with the attendant. The attendant pointed him in the direction of the gold and black Cadillac that had pulled up to the pump. Don put some money in the man's hand and then walked over to the Cadillac. Right away he knew the man was a street hustler. It wasn't because of the way he was dressed, or anything about his demeanor. But game recognize game. Don almost backed off, because he wondered if a street hustler would even know who Pastor Barnes was.

"You need something?" the hustler asked him.

Don needed a lead, so he decided to just go for it. "Yo my man, can I holler at you a second."

The guy finished pumping his gas, then put the pump back in its spot as he glanced over at Don. "You new in town?"

"Just visiting. But dude over there," Don pointed at the attendant, "told me you know everything that goes on around here."

The man looked over his shoulder at the attendant, "He did? Well I just might have a talk with him about that."

The attendant caught the look and scurried back inside the gas station, locking the door behind him.

"No worries, my man. I'm Josh Howard, out of Virginia." Don extended his hand.

The man shook it as he said, "I'm Fleet Smith, been living here all my life."

"Is that so? Then you might be just the person I'm looking for." Don pointed towards the two cars that he and the others were in. "We've been driving around this city for over an hour trying to find a certain street, but we can't seem to find it."

"What street are you looking for?" Fleet asked.

Don told him, "I don't actually know the name of the street. We're looking for Pastor Marvin Barnes. I'm attending church tomorrow, but I wanted to say hello to the family today."

Fleet responded, "I know where Pastor Barnes lives. It's about twenty minutes from here." Fleet then pointed towards his beeper. "I need to make a call real quick. But after that I can take you over there."

"I'd be happy to pay for your gas… for the trouble and all," Don told him, grinning as if the two were becoming best buds.

"I'm good. Just let me make my call and then y'all can follow me." Fleet then went to the phone booth.

Don hopped back in the car with Al and said, "Dude knows where the Barnes' live. He's going to take us over there."

"And you're okay with that," Al asked.

Don shook his head. "No, but we'll be long gone before Fleet knows anything about what's about to transpire. But if he runs his mouth, I'm sure this gas station attendant will know exactly where we can find him, if we need to shut him up."

"Good thinking," Al said as Fleet gave them the thumbs up before getting back in his car and pulling out of the gas station.

"We're off." Don got comfortable in his seat. "I wonder if my son has had the good sense to get out of dodge yet. I as much as warned him that I was on the way."

"Demetrius might think that he got us off his trail by making that call from Concord," Al told him.

"That little act of betrayal from my own child stings. I still haven't decided what I'm going to do with that boy once I get my hands on him."

Al had a few ideas, but he was keeping those to himself.

~~~~~

"A penny for your thoughts," Angel said as she sat down next to Demetrius on the back patio.

"Too much swirling around my mind right now, a penny just won't do it."

"Okay, well then just spill it. Why are you sitting out here all alone looking as if the world is about to come to an end?"

"For one," Demetrius said, "It's nice out here. Back home there's snow on the ground and it's normally too cold to hang out on a patio. But it feels so good out here, we might as well fire up the grill and put a couple of steaks on."

"December is normally pretty mild in the day time, but it does get chilly at night. Now what's number two?"

His brow furrowed. "Number two?"

"You said, 'for one', so there has to be a number two... something else on your mind. You're not just sitting out here thinking about the weather."

He wished that was all he had to think about. But no, Demetrius was actually wondering if he had finally gone too far with his father, and if Don Shepherd was going to do more than put his foot on his chest this time. "Just thinking about my dad. All my life my daddy has taught me that when someone gets wronged, then someone else has to pay. Well, I'm the one who wronged him this time, so just how do you think I'll be forced to pay for it?"

They looked at each other, saying nothing, then Angel began shaking her head. "You don't think that your own father would have you killed? I'm mean... I don't even like my father, and don't understand how in the world my mother could have taken him back and even re-married the joker, but I doubt he'd have me killed."

"We come from two different worlds, Angel. Your father is a preacher and my father is a gangster."

"Different worlds or not, your father is not going to kill you, Demetrius."

"You might be right, but I'm thinking that I don't want to keep sitting here, waiting on him to come find us. I think we should leave."

"Why do we have to leave now? We're out of here tomorrow evening anyway when we take the Johnson's to Columbia. Let's just enjoy the rest of the evening, then we can attend church with my family in the morning, and maybe do brunch before we get on the road."

Demetrius shook his head. "You don't want my father to come here and shoot up your parent's home do you?"

Rolling her eyes, Angel said, "There is no way that your father would be stupid enough to stir up trouble in this quiet neighborhood. Don Shepherd don't want no trouble with the Winston-Salem police department."

"Go get your stuff, Angel. And tell the Johnson's we are heading out. I don't want to be here when my father and his crew show up."

Angel stood up and stomped her foot. "Now you listen to me, Demetrius Shepherd. I'm not going to be running away from your daddy for the rest of my life. And you don't even care about the fact that I haven't seen my brother in three years."

"I do care. I'm the one who brought you back home, remember?"

"But my brother isn't here. Ronny is on a missions trip with the church and they won't get back until tomorrow. I just can't leave before I get a chance to see him. He starts college next year and then who knows when I'll be able to see him again."

He was shaking in his boots at the thought of facing off with his daddy, but Angel wasn't afraid. This girl was tough as nails. He remembered how she spat in Frankie's face even after the man had shoved and punched her in that alley. But if he and Mo hadn't shown up, Frankie would have hurt her, and that's the part that Angel didn't seem to get.

Demetrius may have rescued her from Frankie, but he had never been able to rescue himself from Don Shepherd, and didn't think he was suddenly going to be able to do it this weekend. Why hadn't his father just left it alone? He told him that Coach didn't want the money anymore.

"You know something, Demetrius? I listened to my parent's prayers. And even though I haven't been living right, I believe that God is bigger and badder than Don Shepherd. So, just chill because I'm not going anywhere."

He didn't even want to discuss those prayers. "So, I guess you want me to leave without you," Demetrius said.

"If you plan to leave tonight, then yeah, I guess you have to leave without me." With that, Angel walked back into the house and left Demetrius to his pity party. Her mother was in the kitchen fixing a snack when she walked back in.

Maxine asked Angel, "Everything okay?"

"He's worried," Angel admitted. "His father is not someone to play with, so I understand why he's worried. But I'm not."

Maxine smiled at her daughter. "You've always been fearless."

Angel sat down at the kitchen table. "Oh believe me, I have been scared plenty since leaving home. But after you and dad prayed today, I don't know, I guess some of that fearlessness is starting to come back. Because I don't believe that God is going to allow Demetrius' father to get near us."

Maxine put her plate down on the table and then sat across from her daughter. "You want something to eat?"

She shook her head. "I'm still full from dinner."

As Maxine dug into her second helping, she said, "It's good to hear that you still have your trust in the Lord."

"I'm not going to lie to you. I haven't been to church since I left home; haven't prayed or read my Bible. But I guess I can't get away from all those lessons on faith that you taught us."

"I think your father did more teaching than I did when you and Ronny were younger. As I recall, he even helped you teach those Sunday school classes you did in the back yard." Maxine laughed as she thought of those sweet memories of yesterday.

But yesterday wasn't so sweet for Angel. As far as she was concerned, the whole family had been bamboozled by Reverend Marvin R. Barnes. "How could you marry him again, Mama? Hasn't he done enough damage to this family?"

Maxine looked at her daughter a moment. She then pushed her plate aside and wiped her hands. "I forgave him, Angel. After that, falling back in love with him was easy."

"But how could you forgive him? He made a fool out of you. How many women had he slept with before you caught on? Wasn't one of them a close friend of yours?"

There was compassion in Maxine's voice as she said, "I pray that you never have to endure what I went through with your father. But it wasn't the worst time in my life. You running away was the worst thing I ever endured. Your father was here for me during that time. We both repented to God for our actions. And I truly believe that your father is a changed man."

"I am, Angel. I know I hurt this family terribly, but I promise you that I will never do anything like that again." Her father was standing in the doorway of the kitchen, leaning against the wall. "I never thought God would forgive me for the man I became, but He did. And I pray that one day you will too."

She could tell that he wanted her forgiveness. But her father had broken a trust that Angel wasn't sure could ever be repaired. She got up from the table as she told her mother, "I think I'm going to go lay down with DeMarcus. I'll talk to you later."

Seventeen

"Where is he taking us?" Don asked as Al followed Fleet up a long road that was lined with trees and more trees.

"I don't know, but two more cars just pulled in behind Joe-Joe and Stan, so we can't even back out if we wanted to," Al told him.

Don's head swiveled around. He looked at the cars coming up behind them and his mind went in overdrive. He had messed up and now he needed to figure a way out of this. "How many guns we got in the trunk?"

"I got two shotguns and about four pistols. But there's also a pistol under your seat and mine."

"Good thinking. Let's hope Joe-Joe and Stan are on the ball too." Don reached below the seat and put his hand on the gun. "Speed up and ram his car, run him into one of these trees."

Al grabbed his gun and said, "Sho' ya' right." He then hit Fleet's Cadillac so hard that the bumper was about to fall off. Al then rammed the car again and it crashed into the nearest tree.

While Al was ramming the car in front of him, Joe-Joe put his car in reverse so hard that he slammed into the car right behind him and almost snapped the driver's neck with the force of the crash. Things started happening fast then. Al popped the trunk. He, Don,

Stan and Joe-Joe jumped out of their cars and Al threw the guns at each of them.

Two more cars came up the pathway, but Don was ready for the fight. Taking a negro down was the kind of thing he lived for. "Come on wit' it," Don screamed as he shot off a few rounds. His crew then escaped behind the mounds of trees, determined to camouflage themselves until they had taken out each and every sucka that dared to come against them.

~~~~

Don Shepherd wasn't nobody's joke. He'd won many fights in the boxing ring and on the streets. None of the hustlers in his hometown would have been foolish enough to try an ambush like this. But he wasn't at home; and he wasn't just fighting against these street thugs who thought they could get off a quick robbery today.

Don Shepherd's only problem right now was that when he was done fighting against these men, God's angels were on the scene and they had next.

"The mission is clear." Seth, the mighty warrior had fought against the enemy and his demons on many occasions. He'd only retreated once, and that had been because the Lord had said, 'enough'. "He must not continue on to Pastor Barnes' home."

"It ends now," another angel responded as he held up his mighty sword.

Pop, pop, pop, pop, pop! Gun fire was going off and bodies were dropping.

"We better hurry, he'll be done with those thieves in short order and then back on the road to find Pastor Marvin's home," Seth told the angel of destruction.

The angel of destruction then lifted his sword and began twirling it in the air. Dust swirled around until a wind storm swept through the city that was so strong the electricity was knocked out in several areas as poll lines were uprooted.

~~~~

"I think we got all of 'em," Al said.

"I'm hit," Stan hollered.

"Hold your fire." Don lifted his hands. "We need to find Stan and get out of here." Don was pretty sure that they'd taken care of business. He listened for footsteps as they made their way to Stan. But he hadn't heard anything since he put a bullet in one of 'em and then watched from his spot between the trees as three guys shot off their guns, then made a run for their car and took off. They found out the hard way that Don Shepherd's crew wasn't no easy prey.

"Where you get hit at?" Joe-Joe hollered as they tried to find Stan.

"It's my leg," Stan yelled back. "Somebody shot me in the leg."

"Okay, I see you. I'm almost there," Al told him. But that's when the dust kicked up as if it was circling around them. If the dust wasn't bad enough, the wind started raging and blowing everything every which way.

"What's going on? I can't even see what's right in front of me," Don yelled.

"Me either, Joe-Joe said.

"Keep talking Stan. We can't see you," Don told him as he soldiered his way through the winds and the dust. "We all came in here and we are all leaving back out."

"I know you got me, Don. I'm not worried about it. But this dust is crazy. I can't see y'all either."

"How does your leg feel," Al asked, they were trying to keep him talking, hoping that he wouldn't pass out.

"I ain't never been shot in my leg before. It stings like I don't know what."

"Just be thankful they didn't put a bullet in your head. Because I'm positive that that's what them young guns brought us back here to do," Don said as they kept walking, trying to find Stan. The wind was still blowing harshly, but the dust was letting up.

"Yeah, but we showed them," Stan tried to laugh, but the pain in his leg got the better of him and it sounded more like the whimper of a wounded animal.

"It's letting up. We're coming. Just hold on," Joe-Joe told his friend.

No sooner than those words were out of Joe-Joe's mouth, from out of nowhere a tree uprooted and came at them like a torpedo. "What the dev-" Before Don could finish his sentence he was on the ground, knocked unconscious with a thick tree branch pinning him to the ground.

~~~~

When the electricity went out in the Barnes' home, Demetrius wished he had taken his own advice and got out of Winston-Salem. Pastor Marvin had a battery operated radio, and from what they were hearing on the news, strong gusts of wind had knocked power lines down all over town. It was being estimated that some neighborhoods would be without power for up to four days, while Duke Energy assessed the situation.

Demetrius slept with one eye open, and with every creek of the floor or sway of the trees, his heart danced around in his chest. He'd never been so terrified in his life. But by morning, even though the lights still hadn't come back on, the sun brought him comfort and he was able to pretend as if nothing bothered him as he drove everyone to church that morning.

From the back seat Coach asked, "How'd you sleep?"

"I slept so good, for a minute there I thought I was in my own bed," Demetrius lied through his teeth.

"I wish I could have slept like that," Coach told him. "I was jumpy all night. Any little bit of noise I heard, had me reaching for my pistol."

"Me too," Demetrius sheepishly smiled as he admitted the truth.

"I knew he was scared, but I wasn't gon' bust him out to Coach while he was trying to sound all brave," Angel told the group.

"You're learning early, dear. The best thing a wife can do for her husband is to learn when to speak, when to say nothing and when to pray," Katherine told her.

"You tell her Mrs. Johnson. These young women don't know how to treat no man."

"Whatever," Angel said and then twisted her lip while staring at Demetrius.

The mood was light in the car. In truth they were all just thankful to be alive. Coach even turned to Katherine and said, "I'm glad that I'm able to go to church with you this morning. Once we get settled in our new home, I promise that we will find a church that we can attend together."

You would have thought he just promised to buy her a big diamond ring or a mansion, but actually he promised something much more important. Her eyes lit with astonishment. "You really mean it, Sam?"

He squeezed her hand. "I mean it. You've been going to church by yourself for too many years now. It's time for me to do right by you like I promised on our wedding day."

Katherine put her head on Johnson's shoulder as they rode the rest of the way to the church.

It was the cutest thing Angel had ever seen. She only hoped that the love she and Demetrius had for each other would survive the test of time.

"What's on your mind?" Demetrius asked Angel as he pulled into the church parking lot.

"Oh, just wondering if I could possibly love you more than I do right now."

"We've got a lot of years ahead of us and I sure don't want you to love me less. So, we need to work on that." Demetrius pulled Angel close to him and kissed her like he was trying to make that love grow right now.

"Come on, Katherine, we need to get out of this car and leave these young love birds alone." They got out of the car and went into the church.

Angel pushed Demetrius away. "We are in the parking lot of my father's church, control yourself." She opened the door. "Let me get DeMarcus. You might need to sit here and cool off before you come inside."

"Don't blame me, you got me all worked up with all that talk about love." Demetrius got out of the car, took DeMarcus out of his car seat and then handed him to Angel.

With a new bounce to her step, Angel told him, "My brother should be here in about an hour. I can't wait to see him."

No matter the way it all transpired, Demetrius was glad that he brought Angel to see her family. He didn't know if he would be able to go back to his home after what he'd pulled off against his father. But wherever he laid his head, he wanted Angel to be there. He held open the door and let her walk into the church. But as he attempted to go in behind her, someone put a hand on his shoulder and pulled him back.

Demetrius balled his fist, ready to give as good as he got. But Joe-Joe told him, "Boy put your fist down, this is serious business."

"I'm not letting you take Coach Johnson out of here." Joe-Joe had been with his father's crew since Demetrius was a kid. The man was like an uncle to him, but he was still about to get a beat down if he thought Demetrius was going to back up and just let them bum rush this church.

"It's your daddy, he's not doing good. I need you to come with me?"

Demetrius wasn't falling for it. "Y'all just want me out of the way so you can bust up in the church and drag Coach out here. I'm not having it."

Joe-Joe gripped Demetrius' arm as he showed him the gun in his belt. "I don't have all day to play games with you. Now your daddy might die at any minute, so I need to get you to him. Got me?"

"I got you," Demetrius said as he walked away from the church with Joe-Joe.

Eighteen

Joe-Joe drove him to a motel on the other side of town. They pulled into the lot and drove to the back. The motel had outside doors so they didn't have to walk through a lobby or be seen by the hotel clerk. "Why are we here? I thought you said my father was hurt?"

"He is, but because of circumstances beyond our control, we couldn't take him to the hospital, but he's being cared for, believe that." Joe-Joe looked as if he would do great bodily harm to anyone who dared stop him from getting Don Shepherd what he needed.

"Where is he?" Demetrius asked, figuring he was being set up for some sort of ambush. He only hoped that Coach Johnson and Angel had realized by now that he'd gotten snatched up and that they had then gotten ghost.

Joe-Joe pointed towards a door, he then grabbed Demetrius' arm and looked him in the eye. "Don't upset him anymore than you already have."

Offended, Demetrius said, "I didn't do anything to him. I asked him to stop pursuing Coach Johnson… told him Coach didn't want the money anymore, but he wouldn't listen."

"Yeah, yeah, yeah. You're perfect in all of this, and it's the rest of us that's wrong. You better be glad that you're Don's son or I'd be helping you understand the hustler's code real good right about now." He shoved him, and turned his head as if he couldn't stand the sight of Demetrius. "Get on in there and at least have the decency to pay your respects."

What was he talking about? He sounded like his father was at death's door? Don would never leave him alone. The man had always been around, telling him what to do and what not to do. Who to date, who not to date. He had tried to control his life for so long that Demetrius hadn't even noticed how desensitized he had become to the evil things his father had done... until he turned his sights on Coach Johnson.

Demetrius knocked on the door and stood back. He expected to see his father on the other end of that door, standing there with a menacing look on his face. Then Don would most likely punch him.

He did receive a menacing look as the door opened, but it was from Al. "Well the prodigal has returned. Welcome back Judas, how was the Bahamas?"

Demetrius wasn't in the mood. And he sure wasn't going to apologize to Al for lying about going to the Bahamas, not when Al was lying in wait for Coach. "Get out of my way, man. I came to see my father."

As Al stepped aside, Demetrius' attitude changed quickly. There were too beds in the room. Stan was on one of them with his leg bandaged and sweat dripping off his body like it was raining in here. But that wasn't the worst of what he saw, because his father was in the other bed.

Don Shepherd had always seemed larger than life too him. Don was the Incredible Hulk while everyone else was Peewee Herman.

But he looked so pale and weak as he laid in that bed gasping for air. A man in a white lab coat was putting a needle in Stan's arm and his father was being attended to by some woman who looked scared out of her wits.

Suddenly, Demetrius was a kid again, looking up to his father and wanting nothing more than to be near him. He rushed to Don's side. "Daddy, Daddy, can you hear me?"

"Step back and let the doctor and his nurse do their job," Al warned.

Demetrius swung back around to Al. "He needs to be in a hospital?"

"How do you suppose we get him there without getting him arrested, Genius?" Demetrius stared at his father as Al continued, "If you see Don and Stan down like this, you got to know that the other guys didn't make it."

Al pointed toward Stan. "Why you think I dug that bullet out of his leg myself? Now Stan done caught an infection."

"Did my father get shot too?" What had these guys gotten themselves into?

"A tree fell on him."

Demetrius turned towards the doctor and asked, "How does it look, doc? You think you can fix him up."

Clearing his throat, the doctor pointed toward Stan, "I just gave him an antibiotic. His fever should start going down." Then he looked over at Don and said, "And I've done all I can for your father, but if he doesn't get to a hospital soon, I'm not sure that he will make it through the night."

"Why you think you here, Doc?" Al waved his gun around. "You better hope he makes it, because if he don't, you might not make it home for dinner either."

"This is ridiculous," Demetrius turned on Al. "What did you do? Kidnap these two from a hospital, and now you've got the nerve to threaten their lives if they can't perform a miracle."

"I need to be threatening your life, but Don didn't give the order yet. And I'm not about to let him lay there and watch you die. So, just sit over there by your father and shut your mouth."

"No, no, I will not!" Demetrius wasn't just going to sit here and watch his father die. He wanted to save Coach, but he never imagined that saving Coach would cost his own father his life. Why hadn't he just stopped pursing them?

"Look, Dad is down and so is Stan, so I'm in charge," Demetrius told Al. "You don't tell me what to do because I'm running this show. Either deal with it, or put a bullet in me. Because you will have to kill me in order to stop me from saving my father's life."

Al stepped toward Demetrius, but Don made a grunting sound and flapped his hand. That was enough for Al to put his gun away. "Okay Judas, you're in charge. But I'm watching you, so keep that in mind."

Demetrius turned back to the doctor and said, "No one is going to hurt you. Do you hear me?"

The doctor nodded, but he glanced over at Al.

"Can you get an ambulance here?" Demetrius asked the doctor.

"A paramedics is going to take them to a local hospital. Don wouldn't want that. We got to get out of this town."

Ignoring Al, Demetrius kept talking to the doctor. "Do you know any of the paramedics personally? Is there someone you can call who could drive him a few states over?"

The doctor shook his head. "I'm sorry, but I don't know anyone like that."

"Think hard doctor. If you can help us, I'm paying big dollars. How much do you make in a year?" Demetrius asked him.

"About ninety thousand after taxes. But there's nothing I can do. I'd lose my license if I did something like this."

The nurse said, "My boyfriend is a paramedic. He could get his hands on an ambulance. But it'll cost you the same ninety thousand for him and me."

Al pulled his gun back out. "You trying to rob us?"

Demetrius stepped in between Al and the nurse. He said, "Deal, now get your boyfriend over here."

"Don't try no funny business. Because if he shows up with the cops, I can guarantee that you'll be in need of that ambulance yourself," Al told her.

"Relax. We've fooled around in that ambulance before. I'll just tell him that I want to go for a little joy ride."

The nurse didn't seem to be as nervous as she had been when Demetrius first walked into the room. He wasn't sure if it was because he was in the room, holding Al back, or if it was the thought of making all that money. Either way, he really didn't care just as long as she got her boyfriend over here so his father could get some help.

~~~~

The nurse had been true to her word. Her boyfriend arrived with the ambulance and didn't make much of a fuss when he discovered that there wasn't going to be a play date, but a long drive down the highway. No, the paramedic didn't have one problem at all, not when he found out that he was about to get a ninety thousand dollar payday.

The doctor was the only one who had the issue. But Demetrius wasn't giving him any options. He would pay the man, but he was getting in the back of that ambulance and watching over his father until they arrived at the hospital.

It took five hours, but they made it to a hospital in Columbus, Ohio. Al and Joe-Joe had followed behind the ambulance all the way to the hospital. As Stan and Don were being wheeled into the hospital, Al walked over to Demetrius. "What now, Boss?" The word boss was said in the same tone Al had used when he called Demetrius a Judas.

"I need you and Joe-Joe to stay with Dad while I drive to Dayton."

"Why are you heading home?"

"I'm not. I'm going to Don's house to get the money I promised these people. I'll be back as soon as possible."

Al shook his head. "Don isn't going to like it. You don't need to pay them anything. They should be happy that they're still alive."

"Give me the keys, Al. I'm in charge, remember?"

Shaking his head, Al handed over the keys, and he went into the hospital but not before saying, "You too soft, Boy."

"No, I just believe in honoring my debts. Maybe I got that little personality defect from my mother. I don't know, you tell me." When Al didn't respond, Demetrius walked away from him and got in the car.

Demetrius pulled out of the parking lot and headed straight for his father's house. Demetrius had watched his father open the safe so many times that he'd memorized the combination. So, opening it proved to be no problem at all. Stacks and stacks of cash was crammed into this safe.

His father was greedy. That was the only explanation for why he would hoard all this money while killing a man instead of paying what he owed. Well, he was about to pay dearly today. Demetrius counted out two hundred and seventy thousand, and was about to close the safe when he thought about the ten thousand he'd given back to Coach. His father owed him that money, so he grabbed an extra ten. Even with all of the money he took out, it still didn't make a dent in the load that was in that safe.

Demetrius' beeper had been going off non-stop while he rode in the ambulance. Angel was trying to get in touch with him. But he couldn't stop to use the phone, he had to get back to the hospital. Once he made it back to the hospital, he paid his debt and then sent the doctor, paramedic and nurse on their way, but not before Al warned that he would be coming after them if the police showed up at this hospital.

"Your father's in surgery," Al told him as they sat down in the waiting room. "The doctor had been telling the truth. If we had kept him in the motel room, Don would have died. He didn't just have broken ribs, there was internal bleeding that would have done him in." Al shook Demetrius' hand. "You did good kid."

"Oh, I'm not Judas now?"

"You took care of your father and I have mad respect for that."

"Thank you," Demetrius said, and then his beeper went off again. He glanced at the number and saw that it was Angel.

Demetrius got up and went to the pay phone that was just outside of the emergency room. He wasn't looking forward to this call because Angel's father had prayed against his father. Now his dad was fighting for his life, and Demetrius felt a great deal of guilt for that.

He was no longer convinced that Angel was the woman he needed in his life. What if her father got upset with him, would he pray some prayer of destruction over Demetrius' life as well? How could a man fight against God? There's no possible way.

Angel picked up on the first ring. "Demetrius, is that you?"

"Yeah, it's me. Sorry it took me so long to call you back, but I was on the road and couldn't get to the phone."

"What happened? Why did you leave church?"

"Joe-Joe came and got me."

"Have they hurt you? Do you need me to call the police?"

Where he came from, the police were the enemy. His family would never think of calling them. They just shot first and asked questions later. But Angel's family thought differently. They prayed first and then called the police. "No don't call the police. I'm with my father, he's been hurt."

"Oh Demetrius, I'm so sorry. Is he okay?"

"I don't know," Demetrius sounded miserable. "He's in surgery right now. We'll know more once the surgery is over."

They were silent for a minute, then Demetrius said, "Tell Coach that he's safe now. My father won't be coming after him, so he can go on to his son's house."

"Okay. I'll handle everything on this end. You just stay there with your father." Then she asked, "Do you want me to ask my parents to pray for him?"

"No!" Demetrius screamed so loud that some of the people in the emergency waiting room turned around and stared at him. Lowering his voice, he told her, "Don't tell your parents anything about my father. Just tell Coach the coast is clear and nothing more, okay?"

"Alright Demetrius, calm down. I'm not going to do anything you don't want me to do."

"Good, well… I need to get back in there. I'll call you back later."

"Don't forget to call me back, Demetrius. We have other things to discuss, but I don't want to bother you with it right now."

They hung up and Demetrius went back to the waiting room. His father had to pull through. He just had to. Demetrius could have taken the knowledge of his father's death, because the way Don lived, one had to expect that he would one day get what was coming to him. But Demetrius had spent so many years blaming his father for his mother's death that he didn't want to know how it would feel to be responsible for his own father's demise. His father couldn't die, not now. Not like this.

Nineteen

It took two days, but Don finally opened his eyes. His voice was a bit hoarse as he called out for Demetrius. The nurse in his room heard him and then went out to the waiting room. She walked over to them and asked, "Which one of you is Demetrius?"

"That's me," he said, standing up.

"Our patient is asking for you."

Stan had been released from the hospital the day before and was sitting in the waiting room with the whole gang. "Tell Don that I'm good. I don't want him to worry that I didn't pull through."

Demetrius put a hand on Stan's shoulder, his father's right hand man was like a brother to the old man. It wouldn't sit well with Don if something happened to Stan. "I'll make sure he knows."

Stepping into his father's room, Demetrius could tell that the sleep had done him good. He was all bandaged up, but the look in his eyes told Demetrius that he was on the mend. He sat down in the chair next to the bed. "How are you feeling, Dad?"

"Like a tree fell on me." It sounded as if it hurt to talk, but Don still smiled at his son.

"From what I heard, it did. But look at you. Even that couldn't kill you."

"You mad about that, Son?" Don eyed him, like he needed the answer.

Shaking his head vigorously, Demetrius told him, "I don't want you dead, Dad. I'm the one who made sure you got to the hospital so you could get surgery, so why would you think I want you dead?"

"Guess I just don't understand why you picked Coach Johnson over your own father. That hurt."

"I wasn't choosing anyone over you." Demetrius lowered his voice as he continued, "I just didn't want him to die over a bet that he made with me. It didn't seem right. All I wanted was for you to leave Coach alone, but I never wanted anything like this to happen to you. And I feel awful that it did."

"We needed the money for our next project," Don admitted. "But it all went wrong. I got Stan shot and a falling tree almost killed me."

"Stan is okay, Dad. He had an infection after the bullet was pulled out of his leg, but his fever has subsided and he's sitting in the waiting room with us."

"Good… good," Don said as he closed his eyes falling back to sleep.

The next day, Don stayed awake longer, his gang of thugs sat in the room with him, laughing and catching Don up on all that had happened after the tree fell on him.

"You telling me that the three of you pulled that big ol' tree off of me? I don't believe it."

"Believe it," Stan said. "I had to crawl over there so I could help these two weaklings with that tree."

"You should have seen him. He was all like," Al mimicked the way Stan crawled over to them. "That wasn't the half of it," Al continued. "We kidnapped a doctor and a nurse to take care of you. But that wasn't good enough for Demetrius. He bribed a paramedic to drive you all the way to this hospital. It was something to see. I couldn't believe he pulled that off."

"That's my boy," Don said. Then he asked, "How much did you have to pay the guy?"

"How much is your life worth?" Demetrius countered.

The room went silent. Demetrius rolled his eyes. "Relax Dad, you can afford it. And paying keeps them from going to the cops about being held hostage in the first place, don't you think?" Demetrius' beeper went off. He used that as an excuse to leave the room.

He called Angel back, but as she told him how much she missed him and he didn't respond, she asked, "What did I do wrong, Demetrius? You're acting so distant."

He loved her and wanted to spend a lifetime with her. But her parents had this connection with God that worried him. "I just wish you had told me about your father. He doesn't like me, and you know it."

"My father doesn't run my life, so why are you letting this come between us?"

"I'm not." Demetrius ran a hand over his head. "I mean, I'm not trying to. But I've never been around people that pray like that... and then my father gets hurt really bad. He almost died, Angel."

"I'm sorry about that, Demetrius. But it's not my fault."

His hand tighten around the phone. "I know it's not your fault, baby. I just need to wrap my head around all this praying stuff."

"Okay," she said sounding dejected, "But you still want us to come home, right?"

He hesitated a moment, but only a moment. "Of course I want you back home. Just let me get my father out of this hospital first." He did want them back, didn't he? Of course he did. Demetrius just needed to get over his feelings about that prayer. Her father didn't even know his father, so it wasn't like he had a reason to want Don dead. The more Demetrius thought about it, the more it just didn't make sense. How could a simple prayer cause a tree to fall? And if that tree was meant for his father, then why did other trees get uprooted, and why had the wind knocked out the power all over town. Blaming Angel and her family for what happened to his dad was foolish.

He went back into his father's hospital room. They were still laughing it up and telling tall tales. From the stories Al and the gang were telling, they had gotten themselves ambushed by a group of thugs dumb enough to think they could rob them. That was it, end of story for those guys.

Joe-Joe changed the subject. He told Don, "We need to get you out of here before these folks get wise to anything. Stan has already left enough money on your account to take care of the bill. But do you think you can travel home by morning?"

"Yeah man, I'd rather be in my own bed recuperating anyway. Y'all can always kidnap another nurse. I wouldn't mind that at all. And this time I'll be conscious so I just might enjoy her company."

They laughed, but Don wouldn't be enjoying much of anything until those broken bones healed. But once they did, Demetrius had no doubt that his father would give his nurse all she could handle. Don Shepherd was a menace to society, but he was also Demetrius' dad. Coach had his son in South Carolina. Demetrius could dream all he wanted about being the son of a man like Coach, but it wasn't never going to happen. He needed to find peace with the family he had. And he wanted that family to included Angel and DeMarcus.

~~~~

They had taken his father to his house and thankfully, his boys didn't have to kidnap a nurse to take care of him, because Lisa came running.

Al gave Demetrius a ride home. "We parked the Bronco in your driveway," Al told him.

"Good, I've got to get on the road." He planned to take a shower, change his clothes and then get back on the highway to go get Angel. But as they pulled into his driveway he saw his SUV. It was parked alright... but he wouldn't be driving it anywhere. Demetrius glared at Al. "You didn't have to burn my ride up like that."

"Just following orders," Al told him. "Talk to your daddy. I'm sure he'll buy you a new one since you finally came back to your senses."

Demetrius slammed the car door and walked into his house. He didn't have time to argue with Al. He needed that shower, needed a nap and now he needed a rental car. When his thoughts turned to a rental car, Demetrius opened his front door and stared at the SUV that was parked in front of his house. He had seen it out of the side of his eyes when he'd closed Al's car door, he hadn't given it any thought, though. But it looked like the one he'd rented at the airport last week. It wasn't parked in his driveway, so Demetrius told himself that he was imagining things. Someone with the same type of SUV must be visiting one of his neighbors.

He closed the door and headed to his bedroom. But as he passed Angel's bedroom, DeMarcus ran out of the room and grabbed him around the ankles. "Daddy... home."

Demetrius bent down and picked the boy up. He hugged him to his chest. At that moment he didn't care what anyone said, DeMarcus was his son. He said, "Daddy is home, but what are you doing here?"

Angel came out of the room. She leaned against the door as she told him, "We missed you, I told you that."

She took his breath away. It wasn't possible that Angel was more beautiful than the last time he saw her, but somehow it seemed that way to him. Demetrius didn't know what he was getting into... didn't know if Angel was right or wrong for him. All he knew was that he loved her... ached for her. He pulled her into his arms and kissed her. "I missed you too. I was planning to drive back to North Carolina today to get you."

"Liar." She shoved him. "How you gon' drive in that burnt up mess in the driveway?"

"Don't remind me," Demetrius sounded miserable. "I felt like crying when I saw my baby out there like that."

"I guess you got the message, huh?"

"Loud and clear... don't go against the family."

"Is your father doing better?"

"Much."

"Then can we talk?" Angel led Demetrius to the living room. They sat down on the sofa with DeMarcus between them. She put her hands in his as she asked, "What's going on with us, Demetrius? Am I losing you?"

"Didn't I just tell you that I was coming to get you?"

She gave him a come-on-be-straight-with-me look.

Holding up a hand, Demetrius admitted. "Okay, I was tripping for a minute. But you should have told me that you came from a family like that."

"Like what?" Angel asked.

"All Holy Ghost filled and all. I'm just not used to that kind of stuff. I was uncomfortable, especially when they started praying against me and my father."

167

"They didn't pray against you."

"They prayed against my father, and look what happened to him."

"Okay, so what does all this mean? You don't want to be with me because I don't come from a family of thugs?" Angel asked, getting a bit agitated.

"To tell you the truth, I can't imagine being with anyone else. But I don't want to be with you and then have you come home one day all Holy Ghost filled and praying over everybody and everything."

"So this is real? We are going to be together?" Angel said, completely ignoring everything else Demetrius just said.

"Yeah girl, I think we can make it work... as long as you don't change up on me."

"Why would I change? I love you now and I'll love you forever." But Angel had a Godly call on her life, so she was making promises that she would never be able to keep. She would one day look back on this day and wished that she had walked away... but if she had, the child that God had anointed would never be born and the world would have no hope.

Epilogue

Demetrius and Angel married on a rainy day in June. Don served as Demetrius' best man and just before they walked out to the altar, Don told him, "You picked a good one."

"Wait, I'm confused. First you didn't want me with Angel, and now you think she's a good one?"

"She's the type of woman that you'll be able to count on when you can't count on nobody else. And in our business, you need a woman like that by your side."

"So, you like her because she helped me with Coach?"

Don nodded. "She had to know that defying me could get her killed. But she helped you anyway. I like that. Your mama would have done the same thing."

Angel had won Don Shepherd over, but Demetrius had not done the same with Angel's family. Her father hadn't even shown up for the wedding. But Maxine Barnes was there. And as Angel prepared to walk down the aisle, Maxine was saying, "I know that you're in love, honey. But have you thought about the future? Marriage takes a lot of work."

"We will be fine, Mama. I'm never going to let Demetrius go and he's never going to let me go. He's my match in every way."

"I'm only going to say this to you once, and then I will leave it alone. You were raised in a Christian home. Demetrius doesn't seem interested in the things of the Lord at all. And the Bible asked the question, 'how can two walk together if they do not agree?'

"It's a hard thing to love the Lord and be married to a man who doesn't," Maxine told her.

But Angel wasn't listening. "I haven't been in church since I left home, Mama. But if I decide to go back to church I'm sure Demetrius will understand. We'll make it work."

The look on Maxine's face showed the concern she was feeling. The Bible told her that if you raise a child in the Lord, they will not depart from it. So she knew that Angel would once again serve the Lord. But Maxine didn't have a clue what that would ultimately mean for this marriage.

Angel put her arms around her mother and said, "I love him, Mama. Can't you just be happy for me?"

"Okay hon, let's go get you married." Maxine silently prayed as she walked her daughter down the aisle and God was listening.

To be continued…

Family Business Book II (A Sword of Division) coming in July 2016

Don't forget to join my mailing list:

http://vanessamiller.com/events/join-mailing-list/

Join me on Facebook: https://www.facebook.com/groups/ 77899021863/

Join me on Twitter: https://www.twitter.com/vanessamiller01

Former Rain

Book 1 in the Rain Series

Sample Chapter

by

Vanessa Miller

Prologue

July, 1998

Nina Lewis had the key in the lock of Marguerite's 1990 Chevy Cavalier when she noticed the white Cadillac with tinted windows parked a few feet away. She squinted in the thick darkness of the night as she tried to read the license plate number. The street light in front of Joe's Carryout had been broken for several weeks. A sign tacked to a raggedy old fence across the street read, "Tax dollars, hard at work."

The Cadillac's door swung open. The key jammed in the lock of the Cavalier and refused to yield. She frantically searched for any sign of help. A leg stretched out of the Cadillac and touched the ground. Fear clenched Nina's heart. She dropped the grocery bag. The dozen eggs Marguerite needed to bake that sweet potato cheesecake splattered in the street. The Reese's cup she had been craving for a week violently connected with the ground and her heel, as she ran like the wind. Tears streamed down her face, as she thought, *So this is my destiny; to die like a dog in the street.*

~~~~

The ringing of the telephone cheated Elizabeth out of much needed sleep. She turned over in bed and glared at it. "Somebody better be dead!" she growled, reaching for the receiver. Then again, at one in the morning, if someone were dead, she could do nothing about it. So she turned back over in bed and as her shoulder-length hair swished across her mocha-chocolate face, she resolved to let the answering machine pick up the call.

The salutation seemed a bit long this morning, and the beep was a tad loud. But the noise that bellowed from that little box on her night table was the most annoying of all. "Hi Liz, it's your big brother. You've been so heavy on my mind that I couldn't get to sleep... Where are you?"

"Lying right here listening to you, bonehead!" she shouted at the answering machine.

"Well, call me when you get in. Let's do lunch or something, okay kiddo?" He hung up.

"Not if I can help it," Elizabeth grabbed Kenneth's pillow and covered her face. Ever since Michael became a minister he was always preaching, always telling her that she was a sinner. The way he talked one would think she was a complete heathen who never set foot in a church building a day in her life. Didn't she take her kids to church almost every Sunday? Didn't she sing in the choir and lead most of the songs? Hadn't her pastor told her that he was glad she was a member of his church? As far as Elizabeth was concerned, she was all right, and there was no way she was going to lunch with Michael to have him tell her everything she was doing wrong. Hmmph, no way! Mister Holier-than-thou could just find someone else to preach to!

The phone rang again. Elizabeth sank deeper into her bed and screamed, "Why me?" The answering machine picked that one up also.

"It's one in the morning, Elizabeth," a sultry woman's voice announced. "Do you know where your husband is?"

As the line went dead, Elizabeth looked over at Kenneth's side of the bed. It was empty.

~~~~

"He's out there!" Nina screamed. She ran the entire two blocks from Joe's Carryout. A gallon of two-percent milk was on the hood of the car, which was still in the grocer's parking lot. "I saw him! He followed me."

Marguerite Barrow quickly opened the screen door and peeped around the corner. It was so dark she could barely see past her porch. The street was quiet and full of inactivity. That was one thing for which she could praise God. The neighborhood dope pushers must have checked in early tonight. "There's nobody out here." Marguerite grabbed Nina's shoulders and turned her around to face the emptiness of the night. "See, you're safe, baby. Nobody's following you."

Marguerite's comforting voice was not enough to reassure Nina. She fell down at Marguerite's thin ankles and wrapped her arms around her as if her life depended on the tightness of her grip. "He's going to kill me,

Marguerite. He thinks I betrayed him. He said that nobody gets away with what I did to him." His exact words were more along the lines of, *I believe in an eye for an eye, Nina. You aborted my baby – you gon' wish you were aborted.*

"You're here now, Nina. You're safe - stop worrying. Lord Jesus, give me the strength to help this child," Marguerite prayed as she lifted Nina's limp body from the ground. Marguerite had been Nina's caregiver and protector for several weeks now. "Come on in here and sit down."

Nina dragged her frail, shaken body over to the couch as Marguerite closed the door and sat down in the chair opposite her. Watching as Nina stared off into space, she asked, "Can I get something for you, honey?"

Nina jumped. *A quick death is too good for baby killers like you, Nina. When I'm done, you gon' be the feature story on Unsolved Mysteries.* "No, nothing."

Marguerite's eyes misted over as she watched this young woman battle her demons. She clasped her hands together and asked, "So, did you have any luck finding a job today?"

"No, ma'am."

"Don't give up, Nina. I know you'll find something soon."

Nina looked up this time. A pained smile crossed her face. Her voice was whisper soft. "Yes, ma'am. Thanks for letting me use your car. I'll get it back here in the morning. I promise."

"Don't worry about the car. I'll go get it myself." Marguerite rose and walked into the kitchen mumbling something about washing the dinner dishes. Just as she entered the kitchen, Nina heard her say, "I just wish that child could find some peace."

But peace was inconceivable to Nina as she sat on the couch rocking back and forth. Scared to die, yet at the age of twenty-five she could only think of one reason to keep on living. Life is really funny, she thought. A few years ago she was just three-quarters shy of graduating from Wilberforce University, with a degree in Journalism. She was going to become a world-famous novelist. And out of nowhere, in stepped Isaac Walker.

Sweet-talking, million-dollar Isaac. He had it all, or so Nina thought, and he promised her the world. Only trouble was, she didn't find out until later that it was *his* world he was promising. His world, with his rules and his game board. Isaac always had the checkmate, while the rest of the players stood around as pawns, waiting to be plucked out of the game.

In the beginning, he took special care of her. Dressing her in designer clothes, expensive purses and Italian leather shoes. He even took her to nice restaurants; Not like those college bums she dated. They loved to talk about their future payday while having it their way at every Burger King within walking distance. Nina was sick to death of the "I have a dream" brothers she had been dating. That was one reason she fell so quickly for Isaac. The first time she saw him he was wearing a cream-colored Armani suit that hung on his body like it was made strictly for his frame – and what a frame. Make a sistah wanna SCREAM!

Nina and some of her friends decided to leave the college scene and check out a party on the West side. She had worn her black leather jumpsuit that fit like a second skin and accentuated the curves of her voluptuous boom-boom bootie. The two-inch heel on her black leather knee high boots added extra depth to her five-foot frame. The strobe lights moved over her olive skin as she stepped into the crowded room. The men and women turned to stare as her hazel eyes glistened in the light. Her friends headed toward the dance floor. Nina sat at the bar and ordered a Long Island Iced Tea. Cigar smoke assaulted her nostrils as King Puff seated next to her blew cancer into the air.

Mr. Armani inched his way toward her. His diamond bedecked hands glittered in the air as he sauntered. His suit jacket curved nicely over his muscles.

"Mmmh, mmh, mh," she said while running her French manicured fingers through her short-layered hair, Nina turned slightly in his direction to put out the welcome mat. His pace quickened, and before long, he stood looking down at her.

Honey oozed out of his chocolate-coated mouth as he asked, "Have you been waiting long?"

She looked into those deep chestnut eyes. Eyes that seemed to read her every thought and intent. *Lord, have mercy.* "Waiting for what?"

"A man. Someone to take care of you, like you deserve."

Although a little too bold for Nina's taste, he spoke just the right words to appease her vanity. Most guys never seemed very appreciative. She deserved better. *Yeah*, she thought, *I have been waiting a long time. "So are you here to rescue me?"*

"Why don't we get to know each other a little better first." He pulled up a seat next to her. "Then we'll see if you're worth rescuing." He flashed a dimpled smile.

Nina thought that smile of his must have driven countless women wild. And she was no different.

"If only I had known then what I know now," she said as she sat lightly rubbing her belly, tears rolling down the side of her face. "What are we going to do? How am I going to take care of you?"

She rocked back and forth, trying to come up with an answer. When none came, she put her head in her hands. "If only I hadn't let myself get so caught up."

"Hush child," Marguerite said, walking back into the room. "No since wishing yesterday back when tomorrow has enough pain of its own."

To continue reading click the Link:

http://www.amazon.com/gp/product/B004TGUH3G/
ref=series_rw_dp_sw

Books in the RAIN series

Former Rain (Book 1)

http://www.amazon.com/Former-Urban-Christian-Vanessa-Miller/dp/B004TGUH3G/ref=sr_1_1_twi_2_kin?ie=UTF8&qid=1437950136&sr=8-1&keywords=Former+Rain

Abundant Rain (Book 2)

http://www.amazon.com/Abundant-Rain-Book-Rain-Vanessa-Miller-ebook/dp/B004TGV6WM/ref=sr_1_1?s=digital-text&ie=UTF8&qid=1437950303&sr=1-1&keywords=Abundant+Rain+Vanessa

Latter Rain (Book 3)

http://www.amazon.com/Latter-Rain-Book-3-ebook/dp/B004TH0MB2/ref=sr_1_1?s=digital-text&ie=UTF8&qid=1437950263&sr=1-1&keywords=Latter+Rain+Vanessa

Rain Storm (Book 4)

http://www.amazon.com/Rain-Storm-Book-4-ebook/dp/B004THDQLU/ref=sr_1_1?s=digital-text&ie=UTF8&qid=1437950362&sr=1-1&keywords=Rain+Storm+Vanessa

Through the Storm (Book 5)

http://www.amazon.com/Through-Storm-Rain-Book-5-ebook/dp/B004TM9G6O/ref=sr_1_1?s=digital-text&ie=UTF8&qid=1437950406&sr=1-1&keywords=Through+the+Storm+Vanessa

Rain For Christmas (Book 6)

http://www.amazon.com/Rain-Christmas-Sixth-Book-ebook/
dp/B00AI10TLG/ref=sr_1_1?s=digital-
text&ie=UTF8&qid=1437950470&sr=1-1&keywords=Rain+for
+Christmas+Vanessa

After the Rain (Book 7)

http://www.amazon.com/After-Rain-Book-7-ebook/dp/
B00OJT6X5O/ref=sr_1_1?s=digital-
text&ie=UTF8&qid=1437950546&sr=1-1&keywords=After+the
+Rain+Vanessa

Rain in the Promised, Land (Book 8)

http://www.amazon.com/gp/product/B012LTNJSM/
ref=s9_newr_gw_d70_g351_i2?
pf_rd_m=ATVPDKIKX0DER&pf_rd_s=desktop-1&pf_rd_r=0KXH
ZQX0YJWSDZKN1FMY&pf_rd_t=36701&pf_rd_p=2079475242&
pf_rd_i=desktop

Sunshine and Rain (Book 9) rel.

CPSIA information can be obtained
at www.ICGtesting.com
Printed in the USA
LVOW04s1458141016
508817LV00009B/743/P